01

The
Black Room

the Black Room

BOOK TWO OF THE DARK GROUND TRILOGY

Gillian Cross

DUTTON CHILDREN'S BOOKS

NEW YORK

DUTTON CHILDREN'S BOOKS
A division of Penguin Young Readers Group

Published by the Penguin Group
Penguin Group (USA) Inc., 375 Hudson Street, New York, New York 10014, U.S.A. • Penguin Group (Canada), 10 Eglinton Avenue East, Suite 700, Toronto, Ontario, Canada M4P 2Y3 (a division of Pearson Penguin Canada Inc.) • Penguin Books Ltd, 80 Strand, London WC2R 0RL, England • Penguin Ireland, 25 St Stephen's Green, Dublin 2, Ireland (a division of Penguin Books Ltd) • Penguin Group (Australia), 250 Camberwell Road, Camberwell, Victoria 3124, Australia (a division of Pearson Australia Group Pty Ltd) • Penguin Books India Pvt Ltd, 11 Community Centre, Panchsheel Park, New Delhi—110 017, India • Penguin Group (NZ), Cnr Airborne and Rosedale Roads, Albany, Auckland 1310, New Zealand (a division of Pearson New Zealand Ltd) • Penguin Books (South Africa) (Pty) Ltd, 24 Sturdee Avenue, Rosebank, Johannesburg 2196, South Africa • Penguin Books Ltd, Registered Offices: 80 Strand, London WC2R 0RL, England

CIP DATA IS AVAILABLE

Published in the United States by Dutton Children's Books,
a division of Penguin Young Readers Group
345 Hudson Street, New York, New York 10014
www.penguin.com/youngreaders

Originally published in Great Britain 2005 by Oxford University Press, Oxford

Designed by Jason Henry
Printed in USA • First Edition
ISBN 0-525-47487-0
1 3 5 7 9 10 8 6 4 2

To Janet Dobney, who likes stories
as much as I do

The
Black Room

1

IN THE CAVERN UNDER THE COLD GROUND, LORN WAS AWAKE and shivering. Damp air came filtering down the entrance tunnel and slithered under her fur blankets, licking at her face and crawling across her back. She rolled onto her side and curled up tighter, pulling the blankets over her nose.

All down the cavern, restless shadows moved across the bare earth walls, arching up to the roof and huddling small again as people stirred in their sleep. Only Bando and Perdew were awake, stoking the brazier at the far end. Lorn watched as Bando bent to pick another log off the woodpile. He lifted it up to the ledge where Perdew was lying, next to the brazier, and Perdew slid it gently into the flames. Then Bando bent down, and the quiet, steady sequence began again.

Lorn lay and listened to the spit and crackle of the fire. Gradually her eyes closed and she started drifting into sleep. . . .

And then the noise came.

Scra-a-atch.

She sat up abruptly. It wasn't a loud sound, but it was harsh and unfamiliar—and close. She saw Perdew sit up on the ledge by the brazier, turning around to listen.

Scratch. Scratch-scratch-scrape.

Whatever it was, it was coming down the entrance tunnel. Lorn scrambled free of her blankets and knelt down, putting an ear to the ground to hear more clearly. This time she recognized part of the noise as the scraping sound of branches against earth. The knot of branches that they used to block the entrance was being pushed slowly down the tunnel toward them.

But what was pushing it? What was scratching at the tunnel walls and grating against the small stones in the ground?

Perdew was beside her now, crouching down to whisper in her other ear. "What should we do?"

Lorn waited another moment, still listening, trying to match the scratching sound to something that she knew. Twice before, they had heard claws scraping at the earth around the entrance. And once a hedge-tiger had crouched there for hours, filling the cavern with the reek of its hot, hungry breath. But there had never been anything quite like this.

It started again. *Scratch-scratch-scrape*. Now she could see the tips of the battered, knotted branches moving slowly out of the tunnel, into the cavern. Whatever was making the scratching noise had to be close behind those branches.

"We must wake the others," she said crisply. "And get the blades."

Perdew nodded and shot off around the cavern, quietly and very fast. He tapped at shoulders and whispered into sleeping ears, and as he passed, people sat up suddenly, not blinking and stretching, but instantly alert. There was no sound except a whimper from Bando as he turned to look toward the entrance. Annet cut the noise short, putting a hand over his mouth and sliding her other arm around his bulky shoulders to reassure him.

Scratch, scrape.

Perdew padded over to the corner where they stored the blades. The others moved into position, crouching in a half circle around the entrance, and Perdew ran back and forth, handing out blades until everyone was holding a heavy piece of metal with a raw, sharp edge.

There was one more *scrape,* and then the knot of branches came free of the tunnel, expanding suddenly as the ends uncurled. Bando jumped forward nervously and snatched it up, clutching it tightly and holding it in front of Lorn, like a shield. For a second, there was nothing. Only a steady flow of cold air out of the empty tunnel.

And then they heard another sound.

This one was gentler, sliding lightly over the rough earth. Lorn closed her eyes and concentrated on sounds and smells and the way the air moved against her skin. Letting them make a dark image in her mind.

A soft, bulky shape was coming down the tunnel toward them not moving and changing like something that propels itself, but like something being pushed along from behind. It carried a sharp, strong smell, strange but not animal.

"I don't think . . . it's dangerous," she said slowly.

"Shhh!" Perdew's voice was sharp with fear.

"But it doesn't smell—"

"*Shhh!*" This time it wasn't only Perdew. The sound came from all over the cavern. Lorn opened her eyes and looked around the half circle of tense, frightened faces. They were all staring fixedly at the entrance. Waiting for some kind of monstrous predator.

Slowly, the great, soft shape began to emerge into the

light. It was pale and tall with flat, sloping sides. A long, curved wedge, lying on its back. Lorn didn't know what it was, but the scent was much stronger now, filling the whole cavern. It smelled sharp and fresh and disturbing.

For a second there was complete silence. Then Annet laughed. She sounded startled and delighted.

"Well, I wasn't expecting *that*!"

"How did it get here? Who brought it?" Perdew started to walk around the huge wedge, running his hands over its sides with a look of happy astonishment. It was as tall as he was, and it was covered with a coarse, pale membrane.

What is it? Lorn wanted to say. *Is it food?* But her mouth wouldn't make the words—because all the others knew the answers already. She could see it in their faces. Nothing like that great, pale wedge had ever come into the cavern, in all the time she had been there, but everyone had recognized it immediately.

Except her.

Perdew was using his blade now. He sliced carefully into the membrane and stripped it back, as if he were skinning an animal. The membrane came away easily and the firelight gleamed on long, translucent tubes, hanging one against another, closely packed together.

"Please," Annet said, holding out her arms. "Oh, *please*."

Perdew laughed and reached up with both hands, separating one of the tubes and cutting it free. As his blade went in, juice spurted out, and Lorn caught it full on in her eye. Her mind flared suddenly, exploding with images. Not a wedge, but a different shape altogether.

In another place.

Light light LIGHT—dazzling and fierce—
Brightness. Something round and smooth and cold.
Fingers bent, nails digging in—and that sharp juice, just
the same, into the eye.
Sharp and hurting.
Then the voice, and the hard hand coming down.
Shhh! It's only an orange! Dohfuss! Dohfuss! Dohfuss!

For a second it was more real than anything around her. She felt her brain stir and stretch, like someone waking from a long sleep. Her mind reached out in amazement. *I remember. . . .*

Then something dark and solid clamped down hard. *No.* It was like a hand slammed over her face, stifling and choking, shutting out light and sound and feeling. *I remember,* she thought again, forcing her brain to form the words. Trying to hold on.

But this time *remember* trawled up nothing except the pictures that it always brought. The moment when Zak found her wandering in the woods. The moment when he led her into the cavern for the first time.

Why couldn't she get back beyond those?

2

T<small>OM</small> <small>WENT</small> <small>OUT</small> <small>LATE</small>, <small>JUST</small> <small>BEFORE</small> <small>THE</small> <small>PARK</small> <small>CLOSED</small>. He liked that time of day when it was damp and gloomy, when autumn hadn't quite turned into winter. Helga had been pestering him for hours, pushing her nose against his legs while he was trying to write, but he'd made her wait until his homework was finished.

By then, there was a faint wet mist lingering between the street lamps, blurring the view across the road. It was colder than Tom had expected. As he and Helga went into the park, he put his collar up and pushed his free hand into his pocket, but the mist sneaked around the back of his neck, turning his ears numb. By the time he bent to let Helga off the leash, his fingers were thick and clumsy with cold. He fumbled with the clip, and Helga jumped up and licked impatiently at his face.

"Sit," he said. He took the leash off and felt in his pocket for the whistle he was using to train her. "Wait for the signal."

She gave his hand another lick, almost sitting but not quite, eager to be off. Her eyes were bright in her sharp Jack Russell face, and she watched the whistle intently as he lifted it to his mouth.

He blew twice in quick succession, making a noise too high-pitched to hear himself. Immediately, Helga shot off across the wide expanse of grass. He let her run until he could only just see her, and then he blew again. He had no intention of letting her reach the hedge at the end of the park. If he did, she'd be through it in a flash, into the little woods beyond, exploring the undergrowth and paddling around in muddy ditches. And he'd have to spend hours cleaning her and getting the burrs out of her coat.

He blew long-short-long—*come back here*—and saw her skid to a halt. But she didn't run back to him. She stood where she was, a small, dark shape in the mist, looking longingly toward the woods.

Oh no, you don't, Tom thought. He lifted the whistle and blew again, long-short-long, watching to see what she did. If she came now, that was good enough. If he had to blow a third time, she was in for a scolding.

She turned and took a step toward him—and that was when he saw the two people coming out of the woods.

They were on the other side of the park, much farther off than Helga. Out of the corner of his eye, Tom saw them come around the far end of the hedge and start to walk along the opposite edge of the grass, on the path that led back to the main gate. In the mist and the dark, they could have been any two people. Two gray blobs, with nothing to identify them.

Then the tall one hunched its shoulders forward, running a hand through its hair, and the shorter one tossed its head and laughed. And Tom knew who they were.

Robbo. And The Hag.

As soon as he'd recognized them, they seemed unmistakable. Robert was loping along the path, leaning sideways as he listened to Emma. And Emma was nodding briskly, to emphasize what she was saying. Tom couldn't hear her voice, but he knew those sharp little nods, and the way she moved her arm, stabbing at the air with one finger.

Didn't she ever give up? Tom watched her through the mist, imagining the rise and fall of her voice, carping and criticizing. Jabbing away at Robert with every sentence.

Why did he let her get away with it? He was tall and smart and good at sports. He ought to have had everything going for him. But as soon as Emma started nagging, he seemed to collapse into a pathetic heap. *You've got that wrong, Rob. . . . That's a really stupid idea. . . . How can you be so clumsy? . . .* Why didn't their parents tell her to shut up? Couldn't they see her always putting him down?

Tom had spent years trying to do a repair job. Robert was his best friend—ever since they were four—and he hated seeing him bullied. *You're just as good as she is. Tell her to shut up and get lost.*

He'd actually thought he was having an effect, too. But since the summer, Robert had gone downhill. Tom had no idea what had happened to him during vacation, but it had made him . . . strange. When he'd come back to school, he was like a zombie, going through the motions but not really connecting with anything. As if he was suffering from depression.

It was Emma's fault. It *had* to be, somehow or other. Looking at them through the mist, Tom couldn't bear to watch her jabbering away at Robert. He wanted to creep up behind her and give her a shock. Make her jump and look stupid. He liked getting Robbo to laugh at her.

He was about to set off when he suddenly realized that

Helga hadn't come back. Where was she? He blew the whistle again and peered into the mist.

There was no sign of her—and it didn't take a genius to figure out what that meant. *Sorry, Robbo*, he thought. *You'll have to look after yourself for the time being.* Getting Helga out of the woods was the top priority.

It didn't take long to find her. She was investigating a deep ditch just behind the hedge, and she was wet and smelly and very, very happy. Tom pulled her out of the ditch and clipped on her leash, but he didn't have the heart to shout at her. He just dragged her out of the woods as fast as he could.

As they came through the hedge, he saw the two blurred figures again. They'd almost reached the main gate, but the short one—Emma—was still nodding and waving her hands around. How could anyone have so much to say? Tom toyed with the idea of sneaking up, as he'd planned before—taking smelly Helga with him for increased shock value. Could he make it before they crossed the road and reached home?

He was just about to try, when Emma stopped on the path and started to laugh. And the taller figure laughed, too. Robert's laugh. Tom could hear them quite clearly through the mist.

Then Robert reached out and touched Emma's head. Ruffling her hair.

At least, that was what it looked like. But it had to be the mist playing tricks. Robert would never do anything like that. It was impossible.

———

"WHAT WAS I DOING IN THE *woods*? YESTERDAY EVENING?" Robert looked startled for a second, and then his face went blank. "I don't think so, Tosh. Must have been someone else." He pushed his gym bag into his locker and shut the door.

"It was you," Tom said. "I was taking Helga for a walk and I saw you and Emma, coming out of the woods."

Robert shook his head.

What stupid game was he playing? "It *was* you," Tom said.

He tried to meet Robert's eyes because that was always a sure way of catching him. Robbo could never keep a lie going if you stared at him. Either he turned red, or he started laughing.

But he wouldn't meet Tom's eyes. He closed him out completely. One moment they were having a conversation, and the next . . . nothing. Robert's face was cold and expressionless. He looked over Tom's shoulder and started talking to Joe, as if Tom weren't there.

OK. If that's how you want to be—

Tom turned away and stamped off. But that didn't make him feel any better. Robert was getting more and more peculiar. What did it *mean*? Was he in trouble? And if he was, why didn't he ask for help? What *had* happened over the summer? There seemed to be hundreds of questions and no answers.

But there was one thing Tom did know, for certain.

It *was* Robert he'd seen in the park.

3

"Stay," Tom said. "I'll be back in a minute. Stay."
Helga sat down neatly beside the supermarket door, looking
up at him with bright, sharp eyes, like the most obedient dog
in the world. Tom wasn't taken in. He tied her leash to the
loop in the wall and made sure it was secure.

Then he said, "Good girl," and went through the auto-
mated door, feeling in his pocket for coins. He was expecting to be in and out in a couple of minutes. All he wanted
was a Coke, and there was a cooler full of cold cans right by
the checkout counters.

But it didn't work out like that, because as he walked in,
he saw Robert up at the far end of the produce section.
Looking weird. He was peering down at the brussels
sprouts, sorting carefully through them. On both sides of
him, other people were shoveling handfuls of sprouts into
plastic bags, but Robert was choosing each one separately, as
if it mattered which he picked.

Tom could hardly bear to watch. It was creepy, like seeing
a tramp rummage through garbage. *For heaven's sake, Robbo!
What's the big deal? They're only sprouts!*

At last, Robert dropped a few sprouts into a bag and
turned around to hand them to someone else. And that
was when Tom saw Emma. He hadn't noticed her before
because she'd been over by the fruit, but as soon as Robert

turned, she was there, holding out a basket. Waiting for Robert to put in the sprouts.

Her long red hair gleamed as she tossed it back over her shoulders, and her finger stabbed the air. Without hesitating, Robert went where she pointed, crossing from the vegetables to the fruit and bending over the bunches of grapes.

What order was Emma giving him now? Tom wanted to yell down the length of the shop. *She's only your sister, not your boss!* Why did he always obey her? He didn't even try to argue. He just picked something out of the display of grapes and put it into a bag to drop in Emma's basket.

And she smiled that smug, superior smile of hers and turned to point at something else.

Tom couldn't just stand and watch. Robbo was his best friend—and he needed rescuing. Emma ran her fingers through her hair, and Tom glared as it fell back onto her shoulders in a great cascade of orange-gold.

Robert handed over the grapes, and the two of them walked past the rest of the fruit and around into the next aisle. Forgetting about his Coke, Tom was drawn after them, hurrying through the produce to put his head around the shelves at the end.

They were a little way down the next aisle. Emma was still talking, and this time Tom was close enough to catch the words. They took him by surprise. She wasn't using the chilly, domineering voice he'd expected.

"What do you want me to *do*?" she said. "We can't *buy* any less than that!" She sounded frazzled and exasperated, as if her patience was running out.

"OK," Robert said mildly. "It's no big deal."

Robert turned back, bending down to take something off a low shelf. As he stood up again, Tom waved from the end of the aisle and made the best hag face he could, crossing his eyes and wrenching his bottom jaw sideways.

It was an old game of theirs. The face meant, *Watch out! Watch out! There's a hag about!* And Robert was supposed to answer by blowing out his cheeks and pulling down the corners of his eyes.

But he didn't make the face.

"Hi, Tosher," he said loudly.

Emma jumped and whipped around, as if she'd been caught shoplifting. Then she tried to look casual. "Oh," she said. "It's you."

"Your lucky day." Tom took a few steps nearer, giving her his most annoying grin.

Emma looked at him warily, holding her basket behind her back. "What are you doing in here?"

"They called me in." Tom smiled again, sarcastically. "To give advice about how to appeal to teenagers."

"*Very* funny." Emma scowled at him.

Tom was getting into his stride now. Her scowl inspired him. "I'm getting them to install *Game Show Shopping*. So everything whizzes past on moving shelves, and you zap what you want with a remote control." He stepped neatly around Emma and grabbed the edge of the basket. "Just think of it! No more walking up and down. Just—*ZAP*! And there's your—"

He looked into the basket, meaning to reel off a list of her shopping. But the sight of it startled him into silence.

All she had was a tiny bunch of grapes—four of them—a

little packet of mixed nuts, and three brussels sprouts in a plastic bag. There was nothing else, except the bag of colored cotton balls that Robert had just picked off the shelf.

Tom stopped in mid-sentence, staring.

"Finished making up stories, then?" Emma twitched the basket away from him and marched off down the aisle, heading for the checkout. "Come on, Rob," she said over her shoulder.

"Come on, Rob!" Tom made a face and tossed his head affectedly, running his fingers through a mane of imaginary hair. He'd always been able to imitate her voice perfectly. It was the one thing that was guaranteed to make Robert laugh.

Not this time, though. It didn't even raise a smile. Robert frowned and shook his head impatiently. "I'm sick of all that stuff, Tosh. She's all right really, you know."

"All right?" Tom stared. "The *Hag*?"

"Don't call her that!" Robert said sharply. "She's OK."

"You *are* joking," Tom said. "Aren't you?"

"No. I'm not." Robert's eyes were steady. He turned away and went after Emma, leaving Tom speechless.

That was the last thing he'd expected. He'd never seen Robert like that before. It was like hearing one of the Three Little Pigs defending the Big Bad Wolf. *He's all right when you get to know him. He's even invited us over to dinner next week.*

His brain was working overtime as he went back to grab his Coke. What was going on? He'd gone blundering in to cheer Robert up, to try to jolly him out of depression— and he'd found himself facing a new, determined Robert who argued with everything and thought Emma was "OK."

What did it mean?

He went to the nearest register and lined up to pay for his Coke. By the time he left the store, Robert and Emma were already walking out of the parking lot. He untied Helga and set off slowly, being careful not to catch up with them. He assumed they were going to turn right and take the direct route back to their house.

But they didn't. They kept straight on down the road. Which meant they were going the long way around.

Through the park.

Even then, Tom didn't really *plan* to follow them. But his feet seemed to make the decision on their own. He dawdled along behind them, keeping Helga on a short leash and staying out of sight.

They were a couple of minutes ahead by the time he turned off the road, into the little woods at the end of the park. He could hear them around the next turn in the path, talking in whispers as they walked toward the hedge. When they reached it, they stopped and turned off the path. Tom pulled Helga to a standstill and crouched down with his hand on her muzzle, peering through the bushes.

He caught a glimpse of the orange supermarket bag that Robert was carrying, and for a second, he saw Emma, picking her way through the undergrowth. She and Robert seemed to be following the ditch along the back of the hedge.

Helga butted at Tom's leg, complaining about being held still. He felt around in his pocket for a biscuit and broke it into little pieces, feeding it to her, bit by bit, to keep her quiet. He could hear Robert and Emma muttering softly to each other, but he couldn't see them anymore. They seemed to have stopped, somewhere along the ditch.

Helga was getting more and more restless. But just when he thought he would have to let her go, there was a rustle from the hedge and he heard Emma's voice. The next moment, he saw them both, heading back along the ditch. Robert was screwing up the orange bag and pushing it into his pocket. It looked empty.

So what had happened to the grapes? And to those three precious sprouts that he'd chosen so carefully?

Tom tickled Helga's ears to distract her for a few seconds, while Robert and Emma went out through the hedge and into the park. Then he stood up.

"Come on," he whispered. "Let's see if we can find out what they were doing."

Helga swallowed the last of the biscuit and barked twice, excitedly.

"Shhh!" Tom tapped her nose to tell her to be quiet. He stepped off the path and turned left along the ditch, looking for something out of place. He didn't find anything startling, but he did find a place where the plants between the ditch and the hedge were flattened, as though someone had waited there for a while. Had they dumped the groceries into the ditch? He crouched on the edge and squinted down into its muddy, overgrown depths, holding Helga's collar tightly. But there was nothing except water and mud. Not even a piece of trash.

OK. So there must be something on the other side of the ditch. He stepped over it and knelt by the hedge bank, keeping Helga next to him. She struggled and whined, trying to get free.

"Quiet," Tom said. "Good girl. I'll let you run in a minute."

He bent down to peer under the hedge, but there was nothing there, either, only a thick brown litter of fallen leaves over the cold earth. If this was the place where Robert and Emma had stopped, whatever they'd brought in the shopping bag seemed to have vanished completely.

What had they done with it?

It was Helga who found the hole.

It was no bigger than Tom's thumbnail—the kind of hole that a shrew might make. There were dozens of others like it, all along the bank, but this hole was right in front of the place where the plants were flattened. When Helga leaned forward to sniff it, she dislodged some of the leaves that shielded the entrance.

And there was something underneath one of the leaves.

"Who-oa!" Tom hauled her back, wrapping an arm around her wriggling body to keep her still. "Hang on there. Let me see." With his free hand, very gently, he lifted the other leaves away.

Underneath them was a miniature wood stack. There were dozens and dozens of pieces of broken twig—maybe a hundred—piled neatly one on top of the other, in rows.

Tom stared. He hadn't been looking for anything like that, but it was too odd to be a coincidence. He inspected the hole next to the stack.

It was much the same as all the other holes. But when he

looked closer, he could see that the earth around it was smoother than the rest of the bank. It was only a tiny patch, but when he touched it with one finger, he could feel the difference. The little clods of earth had been broken down into a fine, soft dust.

Helga began to whine, pushing at his hand so that it knocked against the little stack of twigs, dislodging two of them. Tom knew he ought to take her home and come back later on his own. But he couldn't wait. That little hole in the hedge bank was the key to all Robert's weird behavior. Helga would have to put up with being tied to a bush.

She didn't like it. As soon as she realized what he was going to do, she started to whine and complain. But Tom hardened his heart and tied the leash to a strong bush a safe distance away. Then he went back to the hedge bank.

The light was just starting to fail, and the woods had an edgy, dangerous feel. He crouched down and peered at the bank, running his fingers very lightly over the cold, damp earth. It took him a few moments to find the telltale patch of smooth earth around the hole, but once his fingers had recognized it, his eyes found it, too. He bent over and ran his forefinger around it again. Then he slid the finger in as far as it would go.

He couldn't feel anything except the sides of a narrow tunnel, worn smooth like the earth around its entrance. Standing up, he hunted along the hedge for a strong, straight twig. The one he found was twice as long as his finger, with a little jagged stump near its base, like a rough hook. He snapped it off the hedge and sank back onto his heels, pushing the twig into the hole, hooked end first.

Three quarters of it went in easily. Then it hit some kind of obstacle. He moved it around, probing gently at whatever was in the way. When he pressed, it gave way slightly, with an unexpected springiness. When he pushed harder, the hooked end snagged suddenly, catching in something. Tom began to pull, steadily and very, very gently, and the obstacle moved toward him, dragging at the sides of the tunnel. He bent down, with his nose close to the earth, to see what he had discovered.

It was a bit of dead plant. A little clump of dry, scratchy shoots twisted together into a dense knot. Peering closely, Tom could see that the ends of the shoots had been threaded back into the knot, very cleverly, to hold it together in a ball. He couldn't imagine how anyone had made something so small and intricate. His own fingers were much too thick and clumsy.

And anyway—why bother? *Unless . . .*

Unless the knotted stalks were just a stopper. Something to block up the hole and hide the real secret inside. If they'd really put anything precious in the tunnel, it would be a good idea to plug it. And it made sense to use something that looked like rubbish.

Putting the woven ball carefully on one side, Tom felt around in the shadows for the twig he'd been using. He slid it back into the hole, running the hook down one side of the tunnel and closing his eyes so that he could concentrate on feeling the shape of it.

The tunnel was smooth and regular, with a flat surface at the bottom and an even, arching roof. The stick went straight in, almost to its full length, and Tom was expecting it to hit another obstruction—whatever Robert and Emma were keeping down there. But that didn't happen. Instead, he felt the tunnel open out. The floor stayed solid, but when he wiggled the twig around, its tip moved through empty air.

He closed his eyes, struggling to imagine what the space looked like. He hardly noticed Helga's sudden, friendly yap because his mind was completely focused on the tunnel and the messages coming through his fingers. He was deaf to everything else until, suddenly—

WHAM!

Something thudded into him, fast and fierce, without any warning. It knocked the breath out of him, and he sprawled over, falling sideways and backward, into the ditch.

4

WHEN THE ATTACK CAME, EVERYONE WAS WORKING HARD.
The whole cavern was full of food—nuts and grains, seeds
and dried fruits, fresh green leaves and wedges of orange—
all heaped together on the floor. They still didn't know
where it came from, but if they didn't organize it, it would
spoil. Some things had to be eaten quickly, but others could
be stored and kept for later, when it was too cold to go out
hunting.

Lorn stood in the middle of the chaos, trying to sort and
separate. Figuring out how to make sure that nothing was
wasted. And all the time people kept asking her questions.

"How can we keep these off the floor?"

"Are there any more hanging nets?"

"Where shall we put these grains?"

Why me? she kept thinking. *Why does it have to be me?*
Couldn't they puzzle it out for themselves? All they had to
do was see the pattern—and that was simple. First you
looked at the food and sorted it in your mind. Then you
thought about the space, and how things could move and fit
together. It was easy.

But somehow the others couldn't do it. So she was standing in the center, telling them what to do, and they were
going back and forth with armfuls of food, heaping it in the
corners or hanging it from the roof in nets. Gradually, bit by
bit, the orderly pattern in Lorn's head was becoming real.

And then the scratching started again. *Scratch. Scra-a-a-atch. Scratch.*

"Not more!" Perdew said desperately. "Isn't this enough for one day?"

There was a noisy groan from Dess, and Annet wiped a tired hand across her face.

"We'll never manage," Annet said.

Scratch. Scra-a-a-atch.

"Shhh!" Lorn said sharply. "Listen!"

There was something different about the scratching this time. It was hesitant and erratic, coming toward them very slowly. There was no sign of the knot of branches coming into the cavern. Just the scratching, going on and on and on.

"What's the problem?" Perdew muttered. "Shall I go and pull the branches out myself?"

No! Lorn shook her head fiercely, flapping her hand to keep him quiet. Couldn't he *hear* that this noise was different?

Scra-a-a-atch. Scra-a-a-atch. Scratch.

She wasn't sure what was wrong, but her skin prickled and the hairs stood up on her arms as a wave of cold air flooded into the cavern. The knot of branches had been taken away, and the entrance tunnel was wide open. She felt the temperature drop and saw long shadows leap against the walls as the flames in the brazier bobbed and flickered.

"Something's coming!" Bando whispered fearfully. "A monster!" He stepped sideways, moving closer to Lorn.

"Shhh!" hissed Perdew. "Keep your mouth shut!"

Scratch. Scratch. Scra-atch.

The noise was still jerky, but it was faster this time, working its way steadily toward them. Perdew slid out of the circle and fetched the blades, but before he could hand them around, Annet gave a muffled shriek. She pointed at the entrance.

"Look!"

A huge, jagged beam of wood came thrusting out of the tunnel, thick as a tree, heavy enough to knock them all off their feet. It swung left and right, almost catching Lorn's shoulder. Bando grabbed her arm, pulling her out of the way just in time, and the beam scraped past them, gouging a groove in the floor.

Everyone ran.

There was no time to think, no time to speak. They had to get out of range as fast as they could. Frantically they crowded toward the brazier at the back of the cavern. And as the great beam swept closer, they squeezed past the brazier, into the dark space behind it. On that side, there were no holes in the metal to let out the light of the fire. But the scorching heat was almost unbearable.

They huddled together, flattened against the back wall, peering out at the cruel wood. It moved nearer, sweeping left and right and left and right and left—

Not the brazier! Lorn was screaming silently, inside her head. *Not the brazier! Don't let it hit the brazier!* If that went over, there was no hope for any of them. The burning logs would fall straight into the blankets and the new white floss. *Don't let it hit the brazier—*

It didn't. It swept across once more, only a hand's breadth away from the brazier's metal side—and then it stopped. All of a sudden, the force went out of it, and it fell to the ground, rolling sideways and coming to rest against the wall of the cavern.

For a split second, there was a complete, shocked silence.

Then, echoing down the tunnel from outside, came a deep, deafening roar, louder and closer than thunder. A great gust of cold air eddied into the cavern, and a huge thud jolted the ground under their feet.

"It's an earthquake!" Bando shouted. He clenched his fist around Lorn's fingers until she thought they would break. She could feel his whole body trembling. "I'll look after you, Lorn. Don't worry. It's a tornado! An *explosion*!"

Lorn patted his hand without thinking, concentrating on the noises. Trying to make sense of them. There were more thuds, not quite as violent as the first one, and fierce, deep bellows, like the howls of some vast animal.

Bando's words rattled inside her head, without meaning. *What's a tornado?* But she didn't ask. Questions like that made the others stare.

The thuds stopped suddenly, and the roaring softened to a deep, intermittent rumbling. Shang swallowed hard, staring out at the great, heavy beam.

"We could have been killed," he said shakily.

"That's right." Perdew's face was grim. "Imagine what would have happened if we'd been asleep. The cavern's not safe anymore. We've got to get out of here and find somewhere better."

Lorn stared at him. "*Move?*"

What was he talking about? She couldn't imagine living anywhere else.

"We have to move," Perdew said, determined and tight-

lipped. "And we've got to find somewhere *now*—before it gets too cold to go out searching. There's no time to waste."

For a moment there was a shocked silence.

Then Bando said, "We *can't* move! We can't leave here!" He was almost shouting.

"I'm sorry, Bando," Tina said reluctantly. "But I think Perdew's right—"

Some of the others nodded—and Bando went red in the face. "WE CAN'T GO!" he yelled. "What's the matter with you all? Have you forgotten Cam? And Zak and Nate and Robert?"

Pushing Tina out of his way, he charged through the cavern, making for the long side wall where the great wooden beam was lying. When he reached the beam, he bent over and hauled it out of the way, grunting with the effort it took. Then he crouched beside the line that ran down that side of the cavern.

Lorn had marked the line in the earth weeks and weeks ago, when Cam and Zak set off with Robert and Nate on their long, strange journey. *I'm going home*, Robert had said. *I'm going to find my family*. No one knew what would happen if he succeeded, but the four of them had set off together—and there had been no news since then.

The line was for the people left behind, to help them imagine the journey there and back. Bando had laid small stones on it, to represent the travelers, and every day he'd moved the stones a little farther along the line while the others watched him. Two of the stones were lost, but the two that remained were nearly at the end of the line. A red stone for Cam and a gray stone for Zak.

"Look!" Bando said fiercely, bending over them. "They're almost here. If we move, they'll never find us when they come back."

If they come back, Lorn thought. But she didn't say it.

The others were coming out from behind the brazier now, moving slowly toward the line.

"Bando's right," Annet said uncertainly. "We can't abandon them."

"Suppose they never come?" Perdew said brutally. "Do we have to sit here forever—waiting to be killed? I'm not doing that. If the rest of you won't move, I'll go on my own!"

Lorn looked at his set, angry face and thought, *We can't manage without you.* They needed his speed and his hunting skills. And she needed his bluntness, too. He was the only one who questioned her decisions and made her think harder. If he insisted, they would have to move.

Except—

She looked the other way, at Bando standing beside the journey line, stubborn and immovable. *We can't manage without you, either.* He might not understand everything that went on, but he was twice as strong as the rest of them. And he could work all day and all night without tiring.

She didn't know what to do.

"Well?" Perdew said, hassling her. "There's no time to waste. You've got to decide, Lorn."

"I'm not moving," Bando said doggedly, glaring at Perdew.

Why does it have to be me? . . . Lorn looked away from them both, staring into the brazier. They were both right. It was vital to stay where they were, and it was vital to move. But, above all, it was vital to keep everyone together. Was there any way of doing that? The questions swirled together, battering her mind.

And then, slowly, they fell into a pattern.

She turned around to face the others. "Perdew's right," she said. "The cavern's not as safe as we thought it was. And it's not big enough, either. Not now that there's all this food to store. We do need somewhere else."

"No!" Bando took a step forward, looking horrified and distressed.

Lorn held up a hand. "It's OK," she said. "Don't worry. You're right, too. We can't let the others struggle back and find us gone. So we've got to stay here."

She let the contradiction hang in the air for a moment, waiting while the others puzzled over it.

"So what are we going to do?" Ab said at last. "We can't move *and* stay here."

"Yes, we can," Lorn said triumphantly.

She looked past him—past them all—into the dark, hot space behind the brazier, the space where they had all squeezed together to escape the swinging beam. The answer was there. She stared into the darkness, letting her mind sink down below the brazier and the earth floor where it stood. Away from all the huge enemies who roamed the ground above their heads. Down and down, into the safe, hidden space underneath.

"We're not going to live in this cavern anymore," she said. "We're going to use it as a storeroom. But we won't be leaving here—because we're going to make a new cavern."

Nobody was expecting that. She saw them frown, looking

uneasily at each other, but she didn't care. She knew she had the right answer now.

"We're going to dig down," she said. "No one will be able to reach us then. We'll make a new cavern, underneath this one. And we'll be completely safe."

5

TOM WAS KNOCKED STUPID, SPRAWLING HELPLESS AND HALF upside down. His leg had twisted underneath him, and the back of his head was rammed into the mud. He could hear Helga on the other side of the ditch, barking furiously, but she might as well have been in Australia. He wished he hadn't tied her up so well.

There was no escape from the hard hands that gripped his shoulders. He was hauled across the ditch and away from the hedge, and then rolled over and slammed facedown onto the ground.

"Get off!" he yelled. "Get off me!"

But he couldn't even hear his own voice properly because someone else was shouting, too. Shouting and dragging him backward over the rough ground.

"Get away! You're hurting—"

The arms dragged him up from the ground and slammed him down again, and all the time the wild, angry voice went on and on, growling and raging at him. It was all so fast and so painful that he didn't even recognize the voice at first. But when he did, he rolled over onto his back and grabbed at the fists, bellowing as loudly as he could.

"Stop it, you lunatic—it's me! Tosher! Don't be a fool, Robbo! It's *me!*"

It was like shouting into a whirlwind. Robert was scream-ing and shaking and thumping as if he'd gone berserk. And none of Tom's struggles were any use, because Robert was a head taller, and superfit from playing basketball.

There was only one way to survive. As Robert came at him again, Tom lifted a foot and kicked him as hard as he could, in the groin. Robert lost his grip and doubled up on the ground, and Tom crawled away to a safe distance.

"Bloody hell, Robbo," he said. "What's got into you?"

There was no answer. Only a sound of gasping. And something that sounded horribly like a sob.

Helga had stopped barking now. She was pulling at her leash and whining uneasily as she watched Robert. Tom's common sense told him to untie her, fast, and run away while there was still time.

But something deeper and more dogged than common sense kept him crouching there under the trees. Robert was his *friend*. He couldn't run out on him without knowing what was wrong.

"You could have broken my skull," he said. "And I wasn't doing anything. Only prodding around in that hole a bit—"

There was a sudden, sharp movement as Robert's head came up, like a bull's. Helga stiffened and Tom edged a bit farther away.

"Whoa! Give me a break," he said. "What's your problem?"

Robert took a long, difficult breath. Slowly he pulled himself up onto his knees. "You don't need to know that," he said. His voice was rough and harsh. "Just keep away from here."

Tom could taste blood trickling down the back of

his throat, and one of his eyes was starting to close. But he wasn't going to back off now. "This is a public park, Doherty. I've got as much right as you have to be here. If you and The Hag want to play games, you should stick to your own backyard."

"She's called *Emma,*" Robert said in a fierce, clipped voice.

"*Hag* was good enough before," Tom said bitterly. "All those years when you needed a friend to prop you up and keep you going. Or have you forgotten about that?"

For the first time, Robert hesitated. It was just a second of uncertainty, but he looked more like he used to. Tom leaned forward and spoke to *him*—the old Robert.

"This is crazy," he said. "Can't you see what you've done to me? Look at the *blood*."

Robert shuffled closer, on hands and knees. Tom lifted his head and met him eye to eye. After a moment, Robert sat back on his heels. His clenched fists relaxed, but his face was grim.

"You've got to keep away from here, Tosh," he said. "I can't explain. You've just got to promise to stay away."

His voice was very quiet, but it made Tom shudder. Whatever was going on, it wasn't any kind of game. It was something powerful and weird. All his instincts told him to back off and keep clear.

"Do it," Robert said. "Promise."

Robert had got himself into something frightening—that was obvious. And he was offering Tom an easy way out. A chance to walk off without getting involved. All it would take was a smile and a quick shrug. *That's cool, Robbo. No need to worry about me.* If he said that, and meant it, Robert would let him go. He could turn away and leave the danger behind him. Whatever it was.

But it would still be there for Robert.

And they would never be friends again. Not really.

Very slowly, Tom shook his head. "No, I won't do it. Not unless you give me a reason."

Robert stared at him. It was very still in the woods. Even Helga was quiet now. At the other end of the park some children were shouting to each other, but that was impossibly distant. The woods were another world. Another universe. The air hung around them, thick and silent, and Tom could hear the sound of his own blood beating in his ears.

"I thought we were friends," he said.

"This is different." Robert turned his head away. "I *can't* tell you—"

Tom was even more afraid now. But it was too late to turn and walk away. He'd chosen. And with some remote, detached part of his mind, he saw how to make Robert give up his secret.

"You'll have to tell me what's going on," he said. Quite calm now. "Because if you don't, I'll come back with a shovel. And I'll dig up that whole bank until I find out what you've got hidden there—"

"No!"

Robert leaped to his feet, and Tom scrambled up, too, ready to defend himself.

"It's no good hitting me again," he said. "That won't stop me from finding out. Nothing will—unless you kill me."

He said it without any drama, laying out the clear, cold

logic of the situation. Subtly, the silence changed as Robert took it in.

"Well?" Tom said at last.

Robert shook his head. "You don't get it, Tosh." He sounded weary now. "Even if I do tell you, it won't do any good. You'll never believe it."

That was when Tom knew he'd won. "Try me," he said.

THE LIGHT FADED AND THE SKY CHANGED FROM DIRTY white to a dull, dark gray. The undergrowth lost its colors, blurring into a single shadowy mass, and darkness thickened under the trees.

Robert kept talking. His voice went on and on, soft and even, without any sign of hesitation. Tom couldn't see his face in the shadows—only the little movements of his head as he spoke.

About impossible things.

It's got to be some kind of joke, Tom thought.

But he knew it wasn't. Robert was useless at teasing people, because he always cracked up and started laughing after two or three seconds. And he certainly wasn't laughing now. He was completely serious.

You kept asking why I was different after the summer. Well, it started on the plane coming home. I thought we'd crashed. . . . and then it was like being on my own in a cold jungle. Only it was much stranger than a jungle. . . .

It wasn't just strange. It was totally unbelievable. A wild, elaborate fantasy. It had taken Tom quite a while to grasp what Robert was actually saying. And now that he understood, he was even more bewildered. It *couldn't* be true.

Robert stopped and looked at him. "You're not listening!" he said.

"You're not *talking*," Tom said. Suddenly he was very angry. "I thought I was your friend. I thought you trusted me. Why can't you tell me the truth?"

"I knew you wouldn't believe it," Robert said. He didn't sound triumphant. Just tired and miserable.

Tom felt like shaking him. "How could anyone believe garbage like that?"

The moment the words were out, he wished he hadn't said them. It was very dark under the trees now, and Robert was just a silhouette. Tall and strange and unpredictable. Cars swept along the road beyond the woods, and their headlights threw weird, distorted shadows across his face.

He took a sudden step forward and Helga growled deep in her throat. Tom jumped back fast, out of reach.

"Don't be a fool," Robert said irritably. "I'm not going to hit you again. I want to show you something. Come over here."

He stepped across the ditch and squatted down in front of the hedge bank. Reluctantly, Tom followed him, feeling with his foot for the edge of the ditch and jumping awkwardly across. As he crouched down, he was aware of tension. Robert was watching him to make sure that he didn't put a hand or a foot in the wrong place.

"OK," he said roughly. "What do you want to show me?"

Robert leaned closer to the bank. "Can you see the tunnel entrance?"

"You mean that little hole I found before?" Tom shook his head. By now the whole hedge bank was a single block of shadow. He couldn't make out any details at all. And any-way—what did it matter? The hole was just a hole. How could it be anything else?

Robert caught hold of Tom's forefinger and pulled it gently down onto the ground. Tom couldn't help recognizing the feel of the fine dust in front of the hole. He slid his finger forward until he found the tunnel. It was so small that he could cover the entrance with one fingertip.

"It's *tiny*," he said harshly. "You don't really expect me to believe you've been down there, do you?"

"I can't help what you believe," Robert said. "I can only tell you what happened. *Last week, I was small enough to crawl through that tunnel.*" His voice was tight, as though the words hurt him.

Tom's mouth was dry. All at once he found it hard to breathe. "OK, so you're telling the truth," he muttered. "As you see it. But it's not real, is it? Not the way *we're* real. And Helga."

"I was there, in the cavern," Robert said relentlessly. "With all the others. And if you were small enough to crawl through that tunnel now, you'd see exactly what I did. A space hollowed out under the ground, with a brazier up at one end to keep it warm."

"A *brazier*? Oh, come on now—"

"It's an old tin." Robert drew a long breath. "Punched full of holes to let the fire burn. It takes a lot of stoking because the twigs burn through so fast."

Uneasily, Tom remembered the little wood stack he'd found hidden under a leaf. But that was nothing. It didn't prove a thing.

"Can you feel the heat from the fire?" Robert said softly.

Closing his eyes, Tom held a finger over the hole and tried to concentrate. *Could* he feel anything? He didn't know. And even if he could—wasn't it always warmer underground anyway?

Robert murmured again. "Can't you smell the smoke? It comes out of a hole, a bit higher up the bank."

Tom sniffed. There were dozens of different smells mixed together. Damp earth. The brown, sludgy water at the bottom of the ditch. The wet leaves rotting under his feet. And . . . for a fraction of a second, he almost caught something else. Another, more elusive, smell, too faint to distinguish properly. He sniffed again, trying to make it out.

And then he realized what he was doing.

He straightened up quickly, sitting back on his heels. "It's no good. I'm not playing. You really expect me to believe that you've been in some cavern and met a load of fairies?"

"They're not fairies," Robert said. "They're people. Just like us, Tom."

"*It didn't happen!*" Tom wished he'd never seen Robert and Emma in the supermarket or watched them in the woods. He wished he'd never asked any questions at all. "You've been hallucinating, Robbo. You couldn't have been down in any cavern—because you were *here*. All the time. I saw you at school, every day. And if you don't know that— then you need treatment."

He stood up quickly, remembering how he'd squeezed the story out of Robert in the first place. *You won't stop me from finding out—unless you kill me.* Suddenly—horribly— that didn't seem fantastic anymore. He had to get away.

But Robert was faster than he was. His hand shot out and he grabbed Tom's wrist. "This isn't a game, Tosher. You made me tell you. Now I can't let you go until you understand that it's true." He stood up and stepped across the ditch, hauling Tom after him.

"What do you mean?" Tom said. "What are you going to—ouch!"

His foot slid off the bank, twisting sideways, and squelched down into the bottom of the ditch. Robert pulled impatiently at his arm.

"You're coming to my house," he said.

Tom grabbed at the nearest excuse. "What about Helga?"

Robert just shrugged. "You can drop her off on the way. But you're not going home until you've talked to Emma."

6

FOR THE FIRST TIME IN HIS LIFE, TOM FOUND HIMSELF wanting to see Emma Doherty—just because she was such a critical, sarcastic cow. She couldn't really believe Robert's weird story, even if she was pretending that she did. Maybe she had some reason for indulging Robert, but Tom knew she wouldn't try to con *him*. She knew him too well for that.

He was so eager to get the whole thing sorted out that he pitched Helga into the house without even wiping her feet. Then he slammed the door and left her barking while Robert hustled him off down the road.

Tom's mother wouldn't have noticed if he'd dragged ten friends through the house, but Robert's mother was different. As soon as they walked in, she left her computer and came into the hall.

"Is everything all right?" she said.

She always pussyfooted around like that. If Tom's mother did notice anything, she always asked a direct question. *Have you two had a quarrel? You both look dreadful!* But Mrs. Doherty hovered uneasily, keeping her eyes away from their faces. Carefully not noticing Robert's hand and the way it was gripping Tom's arm.

"Hi, Mom," Robert said firmly. "Everything's fine, thanks."

He stayed in the hall, smiling brightly at her. Not moving

until she went back to work. As soon as she was out of sight, he made for the stairs, pulling Tom after him.

"You haven't told her all this stuff then?" Tom asked.

"No," Robert said shortly.

"She's your mother, isn't she? Wouldn't she like to hear all about your amazing adventures?"

"No," Robert said again. In a voice that meant he wasn't going to talk about it anymore.

He pushed Tom along the landing toward Emma's door. It was firmly shut, as usual, but Robert didn't wait to be asked in. He knocked once, quickly and lightly, and then opened it right away, without waiting for an answer.

"Problems," he said.

Emma was lying on the bed reading, leaning back against a heap of cushions. She sat up quickly, and Tom braced himself for a rant. *Don't you dare come marching into my room like that! You're such a jerk—*

But there was nothing like that. She looked startled and worried. "What have you *done* to yourself, Rob? You're a real mess." Then she saw Tom, and her expression changed. "Oh. It's you. I suppose you've been fighting then."

Tom had almost forgotten about that. But now he saw himself in Emma's mirror, with his eye swollen and his face smeared with mud. And Robert looked battered, too. His coat was torn and there were long bramble scratches on his neck and under one eye.

"It's nothing," Robert said impatiently. He pulled Tom into the room and shut the door. "I just hit him. That's all."

"You *hit* him?" That was the voice Tom hated. Hard and

chilly and superior. The one Emma always used on Robert. *You're such a pathetic idiot. . . .*

"It's only blood," he said dismissively, wiping his cheek with the back of his hand. "No big deal."

"I thought you two were supposed to be friends." Emma looked pointedly at his jacket, and he realized there was blood on that, too.

"We *are* friends," he said. "Aren't we, Robbo?"

Robert ignored that. "I *had* to hit him, Em," he said. "It was the only way to stop him. He was in the woods."

"And?" Emma said.

Robert turned his head away. "He was ramming a stick into the tunnel. Jabbing it straight down. He could have hurt someone."

"So you hit him?"

Robert nodded. "As hard as I could. But it wasn't any use. I had to tell him in the end."

"You *told* him?" Emma's voice went up three notches. It was the first time Tom had ever seen her look shocked. "But we said—"

"I *had* to," Robert said wretchedly. "He thought we had something hidden down there, and he was threatening to dig up the whole bank."

"But we said we wouldn't tell *anyone*. Ever."

"What could I do?" Robert said helplessly. "He saw us there. He knows exactly where the cavern is. And I thought if I told him—if he understood—then I could get him to leave it alone."

"And did it work?" Emma said tartly.

Robert shook his head and looked even more miserable. "He doesn't believe me. He thinks I'm crazy."

"It's not that," Tom said half-apologetically. "I just think—" He stopped short, because, of course, it *was* that. He thought the whole thing was crazy.

"So what are we going to do?" Emma said.

"That's why I brought him here." Robert tugged at Tom's arm, dragging him nearer to the bed. "*You've* got to convince him."

"*Me?*" Emma obviously wasn't expecting that. "What can I do?"

"You've got to tell him what you saw," Robert said. "He'll believe you."

"Why should he? If he doesn't believe you." Emma stood up and walked over to the window, with her arms folded tightly around her body.

She's afraid, Tom thought. *Whatever she saw, she doesn't want to talk about it.*

But she did talk. She turned to face him and looked him straight in the eye. "I'm not surprised you don't believe Robert," she said abruptly. "I wouldn't believe him either— if I hadn't *seen* him."

"Seen?" Tom didn't want to hear the answer, whatever it was, but there was no way of escaping it. She was going to tell him.

"I saw Rob." Emma said it slowly and deliberately. "I saw him as clearly as I can see you now. And he was tiny—less than half the length of my little finger."

Her eyes were a clear, light hazel, and there was a pulse

beating in her neck. *It can't be true*, Tom thought. *It can't. It can't.*

"The other Robert hadn't gone missing," Emma said steadily. "You know that as well as I do. He'd been there all the time. Getting up and going to school, coming home and going to bed, just the same as usual. But he was . . . blank. Like an empty person. Remember?"

Tom nodded, before he could stop himself. *That's enough*, he wanted to say. *Don't tell me anymore.*

But Emma didn't stop. "And then suddenly, that morning, there were two Roberts," she said. "The blank one next to me was the size he's always been. But I knew that the little one was the *real* Robert. He—"

Her voice stumbled for a second. Tom couldn't speak. He couldn't do anything except stare at her.

Emma caught her breath and went on. "The tall Robert crouched down and stretched out his hand toward the small one. Their fingers touched, and they just—just—" She shook her head. "It was the most frightening thing I've ever seen."

Robert reached out and put a hand on her arm, reassuringly.

Tom stared at the hand. Until then, the whole thing had seemed like some wild fantasy, with no connection to the real world. *I woke up and found I'd shrunk to the size of a thumbnail.* It was crazy, but it didn't change anything.

Only it had changed things. Robert and Emma were both different. Tom leaned back against the wall so that they wouldn't see him shaking.

"People see all kinds of things," Tom said. The words came out rough and hostile. "It's called hallucinating."

"I'd like to believe that, too," Emma said scathingly. "It would be much more comfortable, wouldn't it? But it wouldn't be *true*. I know what I saw and I know it was real."

"So you swallowed the rest of the story as well? All that stuff about the cavern and the little people?"

Tom meant to sound scornful, to embarrass her into silence. But it didn't work. She gave him a pitying look.

"It explains what I saw. And the more Rob talks about it, the more I believe him. Because so many things fit in."

"Like what?" Tom said. It was almost a sneer—because what could *fit in* with a completely unbelievable story?

"Like—" Emma frowned for a moment, thinking. Then she grinned. "Remember when you and Rob were doing that badge in Scouts? The one where you had to tie knots and splice ropes?"

Tom tried not to grin back, but he couldn't help himself. He'd been determined to get Robert through that badge. Evening after evening he'd sat with him, showing him how to loop the ropes around each other and pull the ends through in the right places. But he'd had to give up in the end. It was like trying to teach a chicken to do embroidery.

"Well, watch this." Emma tucked her hair behind her ears so that it hung down her back in a long red cascade. "Go on, Rob. Show him how you can braid. Do a really complicated one."

Robert gathered the hair in his hands. "Twelve strands?"

Tom laughed before he could stop himself. That had to be impossible for anyone.

"Right," Emma said firmly. "Twelve strands it is."

She took a fistful of elastic bands off her dressing table and handed them to Robert. He divided the hair into equal sections, fastening the ends with the bands to keep them separate. His fingers were quick and confident as he snapped the bands into place.

When the twelve strands had been separated, he started braiding them together so fast that Tom couldn't quite see what he was doing. But he was sure it was going to be a mess. He looked forward to seeing Emma cut the tangles out of her precious hair.

But there were no tangles. Robert's hands moved without hesitating, weaving the strands together. Under, over, under, under, under, over. It was neat and intricate and complicated. Like the little ball of interwoven shoots that had blocked the tunnel.

That's got nothing to do with it. Nothing at all. Tom pushed the memory out of his mind and concentrated on the movements of Robert's fingers, trying to figure out the pattern.

But he couldn't keep up. He could just see the braid taking shape as he watched. It was square and perfectly symmetrical, with four flat sides, thick and shiny at the top and narrowing slightly as it went down. Robert's fingers kept moving until they had nothing left to weave. Then he took the last elastic band out of Emma's hand and looped it around the end three times, to hold the strands together.

"You see?" Emma said. "He couldn't do that before, could he?"

Robert let the braid fall. It hung down Emma's back, smooth and even—and inexplicable. "I learned it in the cavern," he said. "That was one of the jobs they gave me. Helping Lorn to make the ropes. This twelve-strand one is very strong."

Tom was silent for a long time. "Who's Lorn?" he said at last. He didn't know what else to say.

"Lorn showed me the way to the cavern," Robert said. "She saved my life."

Tom stared at the braid. Then he looked up and saw Robert and Emma watching him. Waiting for him to say that he believed Robert's story now.

But he didn't believe it. He *didn't*. Suddenly he was so angry that he could hardly breathe. "That's just a braid!" he said loudly. "It doesn't prove anything!"

"You've got to admit—" Robert began.

"I don't have to admit anything!" Tom was shouting now. "You can keep your silly games and your precious little hole in the ground. But stop messing around with my head!"

He pushed past Robert and ran through the door and down the stairs, so fast that he could hardly keep his footing. As he wrenched open the front door, a voice was pounding on and on in his mind. *They're lying. They must be lying. It can't be true.* He banged the front door behind him and raced across the garden and out into the street. *It can't be true, it can't be true, it can't—*

He was moving so fast that he nearly bumped into a man coming along the pavement. He had to catch hold of the wall to stop himself.

The man stopped, too, just for an instant, turning his head

so that Tom looked straight at him. His eyes were a clear, transparent blue, as still as water in a well. As still as water that reflects the sky.

It can't be true, said the voice in Tom's head.

But it was fading now. He could see his own face, very small, in the dark center of the still blue eyes.

It can't—said the voice in his head. And then it stopped, leaving a huge, empty silence.

The man nodded gravely and stepped around him, going on down the road.

7

LORN *knew* THEY HAD TO DIG DOWN — BUT SHE HAD TO fight hard to persuade the others. Not for the first time, she wished that Cam was there. No one had ever argued with *her*. When she said, *Do this*, people jumped to obey her. They trusted her to run the cavern, even when they didn't understand what she was doing. It was different for Lorn. She had to convince them.

"I *know* it's going to be difficult," she said fiercely. Over and over again. "I *know* there's a lot of earth to move, and we'll have to shift it all outside. And I *know* it's getting colder and colder out there. But we can't do anything else. If we want to be safe, we have to go down farther under the earth."

In the end, after a day and a half of talking, she managed to persuade them all. At the end of the second day, they actually started to dig.

And it was very hard. Much harder than any of them expected.

The digging was exhausting, and they had to work in shifts, changing every couple of hours. Getting rid of the loose earth was even worse. They had to take it outside and scatter it—after dark, because it was safer then. The air outside was almost too cold to bear, and on the third night, Annet came back white and shaking. She huddled in front of the brazier, but it took her the rest of the night to get warm.

We've got to hurry. We've got to finish before it's too cold to go outside at all. Lorn didn't say it aloud, because she didn't need to. It was what they were all thinking. They were already working as fast as they could.

By the morning of the fourth day, they had made a long ramp, leading down into a pit. Lorn walked to the bottom and looked up at the ring of faces staring down at her. As soon as she saw them, she knew that the pit was deep enough. Because the faces were . . . the right distance away.

"That's the right level," she called up cheerfully. "We can dig sideways now and start the new cavern. Let's get going."

No one even smiled. For a moment, looking up at their weary faces, she thought she was asking too much. Then Bando waved a hand and shouted down to her.

"Here I come, Lorn! Don't worry. We'll get it finished soon."

And he led the way down the ramp.

Now they had to cope with darkness, too. The space behind the brazier had always been dim and shadowy, but once their eyes had adjusted to the gloom, they could see well enough to dig. As soon as they began on the cavern itself, they found themselves working in total darkness.

Perdew tried to work out a way of using glowing logs to give some light, but they burned through too quickly and filled the small, cramped space with choking fumes. Until the space was big enough to bring the brazier down, they would have to be content with fumbling around and feeling their way.

Lorn hadn't realized they would all be so helpless.

She'd always wondered why the others were slow and clumsy when it got dark, but she'd never understood that they were completely lost without light.

The first time she and Annet had gone down to dig together, Annet paused at the bottom of the ramp and then began to shuffle forward uncertainly.

"What's the matter?" Lorn had said. "Why are you doing that?"

"I'm figuring out where to go." Annet sounded surprised at the question. As though the answer was obvious.

Annet's voice filled the space in front of them, hitting the earth in some directions and traveling on, unobstructed, in others. The turn of her head stirred the air, setting up tiny currents that eddied around them, rebounding from the walls and carrying the smell of newly disturbed soil.

"It's this way, of course," Lorn said, striding out into the dark.

"Wait for me!" Annet scuttled after her and caught her tunic. "I can't see a thing. How do you know where to go?"

It was a senseless question. *Because I know*, Lorn wanted to say. She struggled to explain. "Can't you hear the space? And feel it and smell it and taste it?"

"*Taste* it?" Annet said. "How can you taste a space?"

How could you not *taste what was there? How could you not use every message that your senses brought, to understand what was around you?* Lorn was silent because she didn't know what to say.

"Are you joking?" Annet said after a moment.

There was something wary in her voice. A kind of nervousness. Suddenly, something else that Lorn had always taken for granted seemed . . . odd. Another way she was different from all the others.

"I've just got good eyes," she said, passing it off as quickly as she could. "I don't think I need as much light as you do."

But it wasn't that. She knew she wasn't *seeing* the space. Not with her eyes, anyway. It was another kind of seeing, built up by all her other senses, making dark, solid shapes in her mind. *But how did I learn to do it? When did I begin?*

She had no way of remembering. No way of answering the questions. So she buried them deep in her mind and let the others talk about her wonderful eyesight.

AND THEN THE EARTH COLLAPSED.

They had been digging for almost two weeks by then, and Lorn reckoned that they had cleared half the space they would need for the new cavern. She had just finished work—digging as hard as she could for several hours—and she was so tired that she could hardly follow Annet and Dess up the ramp.

Bando should have been with them, but he'd refused to come—and she was too exhausted to argue. She left Shang to deal with him. As she crawled out of the pit, she could hear Bando bellowing and complaining.

"Why can't I stay? I'm not tired. I want to do some more work!"

"Everyone needs a rest. And there's not room for all of us to dig together." Shang sounded irritable and impatient. "Go away, Bando, and let us get started."

Oh, Shang, Lorn thought wearily, *you're asking for trouble.*

Bando went crazy if you tried to order him around. He had to be persuaded. Otherwise he'd just go on arguing and sulking, and no one would get any work done. She stopped and called ahead to the other two.

"Don't wait for me. I'm going back to get Bando."

She started back down the ramp—but she wasn't fast enough. As she reached the bottom, Bando gave a loud shout of rage and frustration.

"That's stupid. I'm *going* to dig!"

There was a scuffling noise and the rough, familiar scrabble of a blade clawing at the ground. Then the steady, soft trickle of loosened earth.

"Stop it!" Shang said angrily. "Give me that blade!"

"No!"

Bando roared and scraped at the ground again—and this time there was a new sound. Not a trickle of earth, but a great, thundering rush of earth and stones. Bando yelped and Tina started to scream.

"Shang?" Lorn called. She began to run into the darkness. "Bando? Tina?"

She could feel them moving ahead of her, churning up the air as they blundered about. They were all shouting together now, and behind that noise was another sound, going on and on and on. A faint, steady trickling.

It was the sound of falling earth, dropping crumb by crumb onto the ground. And it sounded . . . wrong. Unexpected.

"Shang?" she said again. Louder this time, to make sure he heard.

There was a break in the shouting. When Shang called back, she could hear the relief in his voice. "Lorn! Can you see what's happened?"

Lorn shut her eyes, listening hard to the sound he was making. And that was wrong, too. The space around him had changed. She went on walking forward with her eyes closed, working out its new shape.

There was something bulky ahead of her, crawling along the ground.

"Bando?" she said. "Are you all right?"

There was a grunt. Then Bando's voice, sounding shaken and wretched. "I fell," he said. "Lorn, I didn't mean—the earth just came tumbling down—"

His voice was leaking away behind him, not bouncing back from the far wall of the diggings, but disappearing into a void. As he pulled himself onto his feet, the air swirled around him, carrying a faint, disturbing smell.

Lorn began to move faster, stepping left to avoid Bando and then right as she edged past Shang. That should have taken her right up to the back wall where the diggings ended. Instead, she found herself standing in a heap of stones and loose, fallen earth.

There was no back wall. It had disappeared. Stepping over the rubble that was left, she spread her arms wide in the new space that had opened up. The air beyond the rubble was clammy and damp, and it carried the nameless scent she had smelled already. But stronger now.

"Where are you?" Shang said, still facing the ramp. "What's happened?"

"I'm behind you." *How can he not know that?* "Where the

back wall ought to be—but it's not. We've broken through into a cave or something."

Tina caught her breath, and Shang said, "Is it . . . empty?"

Their voices were too far back to be useful. Lorn started to hum softly, catching the noise as it rebounded. *No, not a cave*, she thought. It was too narrow for that. The wall that faced her was less than a dozen steps away.

She tilted her head back, still humming. Up above, the space was bigger and the roof arched high over her head, way out of reach. And when she turned from side to side, she couldn't hear any kind of wall. Her humming drifted away into the darkness, and she could feel a faint current of air moving constantly past her.

"It's a tunnel," she said.

"How do you *know*?" She could hear that Shang didn't want to believe her. "Even you can't see that well."

"That's right," Tina said hopefully. "It might be just a little space. Under a stone or something."

Lorn wasn't going to waste time arguing. "Get Perdew," she said. "Tell him to light some logs and bring them down."

Tina turned and stumbled toward the dim light at the bottom of the ramp. As she went up, she started to shout.

"Perdew! We need some light down here! There's been a landslide!"

There were shouts up above and the sound of Tina talking excitedly. Then a noise of feet and a faint, flickering glow that quickly grew brighter.

Lorn stood in the space beyond the heap of rubble, looking back into the new cavern. As the glow grew brighter, she could see Dess and Annet running down the ramp. Then

Shang and Bando and Tina, huddled together by the break in the wall. And then Perdew arrived, holding up two heavy pieces of wood with bright, smoldering ends.

He came down the ramp, with everyone else from the cavern behind him, the burning logs held high to light up the way. When he saw the hole where the wall had been, he stopped and stared.

"Come on," Lorn said impatiently. "Bring the light through. Everyone needs to see what's happened."

Perdew clambered over the pile of earth and stones, and all the others crowded up to the hole, peering through it to see what his makeshift torches would show them. He turned around and stood beside Lorn, with the torches lifted high.

The tunnel went away from him in both directions, curving into the darkness. It looked exactly as Lorn knew it would. Even and deliberate. Not formed by accident, but dug on purpose.

By something much bigger than they were.

For a second, there was silence. Then Tina started to scream.

"It's going to come through and eat us!"

8

How did he do it? How did Robert make a braid with twelve strands?

All of a sudden, Tom was obsessed with braiding. Everywhere he went, he carried a little hank of string—twelve pieces, knotted together at one end—and his fingers wouldn't leave it alone. Whenever he was on his own he pulled it out and started fidgeting with it again, twisting the strands around and around and in and out. Trying first one pattern and then another. Looping and twining and turning until the whole thing was such a mess that he pushed it back into his pocket in disgust.

It was a complete waste of time.

But Robert had figured out how to do it. He wouldn't have been able to learn from a diagram or any kind of written instructions. He must have found out by accident.

He *must* have.

Tom knew it would only take a few minutes on the Internet to find the pattern he needed. But he didn't want to do it like that. He wanted to figure it out for himself, the way Robert must have done.

It was important to keep his braiding a secret, of course, until he'd worked out how to do it. But it wasn't easy to hide it. Suddenly, wherever he went, Robert seemed to be around. At school, he was never out of earshot. It was impossible to sneak off on his own.

That didn't look odd to anyone else, because people were used to seeing them together, but Tom knew he was being watched. Once, when they were on their own, he rounded on Robert, yelling angrily.

"Get off my back! You're driving me crazy!"

Robert just shrugged. "I thought you might want to talk, that's all."

"About what? Your precious fairy story?" Tom glared and stamped off.

But the next time he turned around—there was Robert. Chatting away to Joe, as if he hadn't noticed that Tom was there.

It wasn't always Robert. Sometimes it was Emma who turned up, especially in the park. Three or four times she appeared out of nowhere when Tom was walking Helga early in the morning. He began to feel as if she could read his mind.

It came to a head one Friday morning. As he and Helga went in through the park gates, Emma appeared, as if by magic, coming down the path toward him.

"Why don't you leave me alone?" he muttered.

Emma shrugged and fell into step beside him. "It's a public park."

"Well, go and infest another part of it." Tom started to walk faster, trying to get rid of her, and Helga gave a harsh, low-pitched bark that turned into a growl. He bent down and let her off the leash.

"I hope you're not going to send her into the woods," Emma said.

That was the last straw. Tom stopped dead and glared at

her. "It's none of your business where we go. I won't meddle with your silly little games, but I'm not going to let them get in my way."

"Look—" Emma frowned. "Try and see it from our point of view. Robert made a bad mistake, telling you about . . . what happened to him. And now we don't know what to do. But we've got to protect the people in the cavern."

"There *aren't* any people!" Tom grabbed her arms and turned her around to face the woods. Reaching over her shoulder, he jabbed his finger toward the trees. "Look, Emma. That's an ordinary little woods at the end of the park. With an ordinary hedge in front of it." His breath billowed past the side of her head, making clouds in the chilly air. "The cavern and the little people and all those things are just fantasy."

"I wish they were," Emma said ruefully.

Give up, Tom thought. *Just give up*. It was like banging his head against a brick wall. He stepped back and took out his whistle to signal Helga.

As he put it to his lips, he saw a movement beyond her. There was a flutter of white, and a figure came out of the woods, pushing an empty shopping bag into its pocket. So Robert was still taking food parcels to the fairies, was he?

Tom blew his whistle quickly. He wanted to get out of there before Robert saw him. To his relief, Helga turned and started back right away. The moment she reached him, he bent down and clipped on her leash. She would have to make do with a walk around the streets.

When he straightened up, he saw that Emma had already gone. She was marching across the grass to join Robert—

with a neat, square plait hanging down her back. It was thick and shiny and perfectly made, the most beautiful piece of braiding Tom had ever seen.

And it felt like a slap in the face.

WHEN HE REACHED HOME, HIS MOTHER WAS SITTING blearily over her breakfast coffee. Her long hair was hanging over her shoulder in an ordinary three-strand braid. She always slept with it like that.

He hadn't meant to tell her anything about what was going on, but the words came by themselves. Abrupt and aggressive.

"All girls can braid, can't they? It's no big deal."

"What?" His mother blinked up at him. "What's up, Tom?"

"Why do you always do your hair like that? Could you do a different kind of braid if you wanted to? How about one with twelve strands?"

She shrugged. "Why not?"

Tom's heart thudded. Pulling the string out of his pocket, he untangled it quickly and pushed it at her. "Show me how you do it."

She looked startled, but she took the string and began to weave it slowly and clumsily. It was no use at all. She was making something like a fat, untidy, three-strand braid. Using exactly the same method.

"Is that the only way you can do it?" he said impatiently.

"If it's not good enough, you'd better do it yourself." His mother pushed the string back at him and stood up, looking annoyed. "I need to get ready for work." She drained her coffee and disappeared upstairs.

Tom was left on his own, with Helga whining for a drink. He filled her water bowl and then stood beside it, unraveling his mother's sloppy, irregular braid. He was so disappointed that he wanted to scream.

He was desperate to see a proper twelve-strand braid. Not made by Robert. Not in Emma's hair. There had to be one somewhere.

When it finally turned up, he almost missed it.

He was mooching around town on his own, on Saturday afternoon. He'd started out with Joe and Catesby, but they'd stopped in the music shop to chat up some girls (one of them with a dull, little three-strand braid and the others with no braids at all). After a few moments, Tom had drifted off and left them to it. He was too restless to stand still for long.

He slouched to the square in the middle of town and worked his way along the shops, peering in the windows and watching the customers. One shop had a couple of braided belts (five and six strands, plaited flat) in the window and another had a rack of hair ornaments made of braided ribbon (only four strands). That was it. There was nothing else. Nothing remotely like what he was searching for. But he figured there must be loads of them around. If Robbo could do it, it had to be easy to make them. All he had to do was find one. . . .

It was almost lunchtime when he saw the boy with the sports bag. He was sitting on the bench by the fountain, in the middle of the main square, with his fat knees spread wide apart. Normally, Tom would have gone by without a second look, but he'd just bought himself a Coke, and he wanted to sit by the fountain to drink it.

But the boy had gotten there first.

He was only about eleven or twelve, with a pale, bloated face and a belly that hung over the top of his trousers. There should have been room for two more people on the bench, but he'd planted himself right in the middle, with his sports bag on one side and a row of little white paper bags on the other. The paper bags were full of candies, and he was eating his way steadily through them.

Dip, went his fingers, first into one bag and then into another. He wasn't taking one sweet at a time. He was gathering them in handfuls and cramming them into his mouth, so fast that he barely had time to chew. *Dip, dip, dip*.

He didn't even seem to be enjoying them. His eyes stared into the distance, and he shoved the candy into his mouth without looking. Without even finishing the previous mouthful. *Dip*, went his hand, into the bags and then straight up to his mouth. And his mouth opened automatically, just wide enough to let him push them in. Then it clamped shut again and he went on chewing.

It made Tom feel sick. He was about to walk away when the boy suddenly screwed all the paper bags together and dropped them under the seat. Then he heaved himself off the bench, unzipped his sports bag, and took out a couple of bills. With the money in one hand and the sports bag slung over his shoulder, he lumbered across the square—heading straight for the nearest sweet shop.

He was going to buy *more* candy? Tom was so astounded that he turned around to watch. And there was no doubt about it. The boy pushed the shop door open, with his pudgy hand on the door and his sports bag hanging against his back.

And on the sports bag, hanging down from the zipper toggle, was a neat little blue braid.

Not a big braid. Nothing showy. Tom wouldn't even have noticed it if he hadn't been watching out for things like that. It was just a little square plait made of blue woolen threads, with a few flecks of brown twisted through it, appearing and disappearing at odd intervals. There was nothing remotely special about it.

But it looked like a twelve-strand braid.

9

FOR A SECOND, TOM COULDN'T BELIEVE IT WAS ACTUALLY there. Was he imagining it? Was he so obsessed that his poor, exhausted brain had started conjuring up hallucinations? He blinked and looked again.

The braid was still there. So it was real. And it was exactly the right shape, even though it wasn't long and golden orange. Neat and tight and square. He just had time to imagine how the pattern would feel under his fingers. Then the boy and the bag and the braid all disappeared into the sweet shop.

He wanted to shout triumphantly. *Got you, Robbo! There's nothing special about that braid of yours. Any old sausage-fingered kid can make one like it!*

That would make Robert think, all right. And it would fix Emma, too. He could hardly wait to tell her. The braid was just as ordinary as the little woods in the park. Once she knew that—once she could see that *he* knew—she'd have to stop playing games with Robert. And start looking after him.

But the imaginary scene in his head started going wrong. Because he knew what Emma would say. He could almost hear her superior, sarcastic voice. *So you found a twelve-strand braid, did you? Are you sure it wasn't nine? Or ten? Did you count the strands?*

And, of course, he hadn't counted them. He couldn't be

sure there really were twelve. And even if he was sure, that wouldn't be good enough once he was face-to-face with Emma. He had to double-check. To get a better look.

He stayed on the bench, waiting for the boy to come out of the sweet shop. Determined to track him all the way home if he had to.

But that wasn't necessary. Because when the boy came out of the shop, he headed straight back to the bench and sat down in exactly the same place as before. He had three more paper bags in his hand, and he put them down on the bench, on his left-hand side, exactly where the other bags had been.

Then he slipped the sports bag off his shoulder and turned to put it on the other side. But there wasn't room, because Tom was sitting there.

If their eyes had met, even for a second, things would have been different. Tom was ready to give him a smile. He was ready to slide to the end of the bench to make room for the bag. He would have done anything that gave him a chance to talk and ask a few questions about the braid.

But the boy glanced away, avoiding him. He just dropped his sports bag onto the ground, half of it in front of his own feet and half in front of Tom's. Then he turned to the sweets and started stuffing them into his mouth.

The braid was there, right next to Tom's feet, hanging down from the zipper toggle. He could hardly breathe. It was close enough to touch. *Don't move too fast. Don't blow it.* As casually as he could, he bent over and started retying one of his shoelaces.

As soon as he bent down, the boy's head whipped around. The pale eyes peered suspiciously.

"Hi." Tom looked up, straight at him. "You OK?"

He said it in the friendliest voice he could and grinned cheerfully. But the boy didn't respond. For a second he just stared, obviously startled at being spoken to. Then he glowered and turned his back ostentatiously, shielding the sweets with his body.

Right, Tom thought. *If you're going to be like that, I'll do it another way.* As the fat hand reached into the paper bags, Tom took his chance. His fingers flew to the zipper toggle, and he struggled with the knot, trying to untie the little braid.

But he couldn't. The knot was pulled tight, and the braiding made it almost impossible to pull it apart.

So he simply picked up the bag and walked off with it.

He'd never stolen anything before. Even while his fingers were closing around the handles, he was telling himself that he wouldn't really do it. But his arm kept moving, and the boy didn't turn around, and suddenly—there Tom was, on the other side of the square, with the bag in his hand.

He slipped between two shops, into the parking lot, and then ran, as fast as he could, heading out of town toward the park and Robert's house. There was one shout from behind him, and then—nothing. When he glanced over his shoulder, there was no one racing after him.

He slowed to a walk and started imagining what it would be like to wave the braid in Robert's face. He wanted a really good punch line. Something smart and snappy that would really maximize the shock—without sounding as though he cared too much. He imagined himself lounging casually against the side of the doorway, saying something short and witty.

He hadn't counted on being angry.

When Robert opened the door, all the cool, clever things Tom had meant to say went right out of his head. He just pushed the sports bag forward and shook it furiously.

"Look," he said roughly. "Look!"

For a second, Robert didn't understand what Tom wanted him to see. Then Tom thrust the bag at him, zipper uppermost, so that the toggle was right under his nose.

"*Look!*"

Robert froze and all the color drained out of his face. He reached out a hand toward the braid and stopped before he touched it, as if he thought it would burn him.

"Where did you get that?" he whispered.

"Don't you know?" Tom flipped the braid with his finger. "I thought you were the expert. Why don't you tell me where it comes from?" He pushed the bag at Robert again, harder this time, trying to knock him off balance.

But he wasn't strong enough. Robert caught him by the arms, pulling him forward. "*Where did you get that braid?*"

For a moment Tom couldn't speak. It was like a horrible joke. He'd spent years nagging Robert to be more aggressive (*Stand up for what you want. Assert yourself. Don't take "no" for an answer*), and now all that had backfired on him.

"Tell me!" Robert shook him again, impatiently. "Where did you find it?"

"Why?" Tom struggled to get the words out. "What's the big deal?"

For a moment he thought he was going to get hit again. Robert caught hold of the braid and flapped it in his face.

"Can't you see how the hair's braided into it? That's what Lorn does. *She must have made it!*"

"*Lorn?*" Tom couldn't make sense of the words. "What are you talking about? I thought Lorn was some kind of midget fairy. How could she make anything as big as that?"

Robert closed his eyes and spoke very slowly. "Why don't you *listen*—instead of trying to be clever? It hasn't got anything to do with fairies. Lorn's a real person—like you and me. And when I was in the cavern, I was still *here*, wasn't I? Even if I was like a zombie."

Tom stared. *I don't want to hear this. It's crazy.*

But Robert's voice went on relentlessly. "That's Lorn's pattern, Tosh. And I've got to find her. If I can't get her out of the cavern before the winter comes, she'll die of cold. So are you going to tell me where you got it from—or do I have to beat it out of you?"

Tom dropped the bag and put his hands in the air. "Calm down. Of course I'll tell you. For what it's worth. I swiped it from a boy in town."

"You *stole* it?"

"Only so I could show you the braid," Tom said defensively. "And he was a stupid kid. Too busy guzzling sweets to notice what was going on."

"You didn't have to *take* it. You should have asked him where he got it from."

"Why would I care?" Tom was beginning to feel annoyed now. "It's just a few bits of wool twisted together, Robbo. It doesn't mean a thing to me."

They were still standing at the front door, Robert inside the house and Tom outside. Suddenly, Robert stepped over the threshold and pulled the door shut behind him. He bent down and picked up the sports bag.

"Come on," he said. "We'll go back, and if the boy's still there, we can ask him about it."

"Yeah, right," Tom said sarcastically. "*Hi there! I'm the one who stole your bag. And now I'd like you to answer a few questions.* That's really going to work, isn't it?"

He turned to go, but Robert's free hand shot out and closed around his arm.

"I'm not messing around, Tosh," he said. Dangerously. "I've got to find Lorn. So either you come and point out the boy—if he's still there—or else I go by myself. And if there's any fuss about the bag getting stolen, I'll tell the police where to find you."

"You wouldn't do that," Tom said, trying to pull his arm free. "Not to me."

"Oh no?" Robert raised his eyebrows. "We're past all that, Tosh. You changed the rules when you threatened to dig up the cavern."

"But I didn't actually mean—"

Robert's face didn't change. Tom had never seen that calm, determined expression before. He didn't fancy his chances if he tried to run off.

"You really want to find this girl," he said. "Don't you?"

"I *have* to find her," Robert said. "Before it's too late. It's very, very important—and I'll do whatever it takes."

"OK," Tom said slowly. "We'll go back and look. As long as I don't have to talk to him."

"That'll do." Robert began walking across the garden, pulling Tom along with him. "All you need to do is show me the right person."

"He's probably gone by now."

"Then we'll go back next Saturday," Robert said steadily. "And the one after that and the one after that, until we find him."

Tom tugged at his arm again. "You don't have to keep hold of me. I said I'd come."

Robert gave him a sharp look and then let go. "OK," he said. "But it's the same deal."

Tom marched along without saying anything else. He just wanted to get it over with. All they had to do was go to the square and take a quick look around. He was pretty sure the boy would have cleared off by now.

But he hadn't.

He was standing over on the other side of the square, with his back to them, talking to a big man with a gray, heavy face. And he was making excuses. Tom could tell he was, even without hearing his voice. He kept shifting from foot to foot, leaning forward to speak in hesitant bursts and then stopping short.

The man wasn't saying anything. He was standing very still, and his face was without any kind of expression apart from a terrible close attention. Whatever the boy said, the man didn't make any kind of reply. He just let the boy go on and on with his jerky excuses. It was like watching a worm writhing on the end of a hook.

Tom shivered and stepped back slightly.

Robert was watching him. "You can see him, can't you?" he said quickly. "Where is he?"

Tom looked at the man's cold face and his narrow, closed mouth. "Don't try and talk to him now, Robbo. His dad's there."

"So?" Robert made a small impatient movement. His eyes traveled slowly around the square until they reached the right place. Then he glanced around. "That's him. Isn't it?"

"He won't tell you anything," Tom said. "Not while that man's there. He's afraid of him."

The man was talking now, but only his lips were moving, like wet, red worms. His face was heavy and unhealthy, like something bodged out of dirty white clay.

Robert watched him for a moment. "You don't know," he said. "Not just from looking. He might be fine when you talk to him."

"But suppose he's not fine? Suppose he just takes the bag and walks off? What are you going to do then?" Tom shook his head and edged backward. He had no intention of going anywhere near that man.

"Hang on a minute." Robert caught hold of Tom's sleeve. "Maybe he'll go off somewhere. Then we can get the boy on his own."

But it didn't happen like that. Almost as he said it, the man did turn around and walk off. He went briskly out of the square and down the road toward the parking lot. But the boy went with him, almost jogging as he tried to keep up.

Robert tugged at Tom's sleeve and pulled him across the

square. But as they reached the edge of the parking lot, the boy and his father were already climbing into a car. Robert broke into a run, but Tom could see that was pointless. He stayed where he was, watching the car back out of its space and drive away. It turned left out of the lot and then right, so that it disappeared almost instantly.

That's it, then, Tom thought. *We've lost them.*

He was amazed at the sudden burst of feeling that swept through him. He could have laughed out loud from sheer relief.

10

THE NEW CAVERN WAS FULL OF NOISE AND TERROR. PEOPLE began to blunder around, shouting and pushing at each other as they struggled to get away from the break in the wall. Lorn tried to talk above the yelling, to get them to calm down. But her voice wasn't strong enough, and she couldn't make them hear her.

It was Perdew who stopped the chaos. He lifted the glowing wood high above his head, so that it flared suddenly brighter, and as the others turned to look, he bellowed at them. "DO YOU WANT IT TO HEAR YOU?"

That brought immediate silence. Total and terrified. Perdew let it register with everyone. Then he looked at Lorn.

"OK," he said. "What do we do now?"

"We've got to fill all this in!" Tina said, not waiting for Lorn to answer. "Put it all back just the way it was, before we ever started digging!"

"No!" Lorn said. "No, we can't!"

She hadn't worked out what else they could do. Not yet. But she knew that they had to be down under the earth. It was like hearing a voice in her head. *No one will get you down there. You'll be safe under the ground.* The idea of abandoning the new space they had made filled her with panic.

"So what *are* we going to do?" Perdew said steadily. "Sit here and wait to be eaten?"

"Of course not!" Lorn forced herself to start thinking. "We've got to do something—but we can't fill in everything we've dug out. How could we ever collect enough earth?"

"OK." Perdew wasn't going to let it drop. "If we can't use this, then we'll have to find a new cavern after all."

Oh no, Lorn thought. *You're not getting away with that.* She looked straight back at him. "You want to go out exploring? In the cold?"

For the first time, she felt a response from the others. She could see them imagining what it would be like trekking over the hard, frosty earth, with the icy air eating into their bones. It was too late for exploring now, and they all knew it. They had to stay where they were.

"So what are we going to do about this hole?" Dess said. Not belligerently like Perdew, but desperate for an answer.

"We'll—"

We'll have to talk about that, Lorn was going to say. But the words came out differently. Because suddenly she saw what they could do.

"We'll build a wall," she said.

No one was expecting that. She felt their surprise—and then their bewilderment. They didn't understand what she meant.

She turned toward the fallen earth, eager to explain. "Bring the light here, Perdew. So everyone can see."

The wood had almost burned through, but Perdew carried it over to her, standing to one side of the hole to light it clearly.

Lorn swept her arm in a wide arc in front of the wall. "We can build a barrier right across this end. With big stones. If we make it thick enough, it will keep anything out—and we'll still have the space on this side, to use as a storeroom."

She saw them nod as they started to take it in, and she knew they were going to agree.

"That would solve a lot of things," Shang said thoughtfully. "If we put the stores down here, we'll have more room up above."

"It won't solve anything," Perdew said. "It'll just leave us back where we started—in the old, dangerous cavern. We have to *move*."

But he wasn't sounding so fierce now. He'd lost, and he knew it. Lorn didn't bother to argue anymore. She raised her voice and spoke to the others. "What do you think? It means going outside to find stones. Can you deal with that?"

Before anyone could answer, Perdew caught his breath sharply. The wood he was holding had burned right down to his hand. He flicked it into a corner and watched it disintegrate into a pile of glowing embers.

"It's going to be tricky building a wall in the dark," he said sourly as the light faded.

"I can cope with darkness," Lorn said. "I'll stay down here and build the wall." She turned sideways, toward Bando. "You'll help me lift the stones, won't you?"

As the last light flickered away, she saw him grin. "Yes! I'll help you! I'll carry the stones—and you can tell me where to put them."

Perdew shrugged, looking resigned. "OK. I give in. Let's start stone hunting. You'd better wait at the bottom of the ramp, Bando, so you'll be ready to take the stones."

"Yes! I'll be ready!"

Bando bounded forward, toward the ramp, and Perdew hustled everyone after him.

Lorn was left on her own in the dark. She took a long, deep breath. Then—once she was sure that no one could see her—she stepped through the break in the wall, into the empty tunnel beyond.

She could feel it stretching left and right, going off into the distance. It was a huge space, bigger than anything they could have dug on their own. The creature that had made it must be vast and dangerous, and she knew she ought to be afraid. But she wasn't. Instead, she felt something strange and irrational drawing her on, like a voice calling to her. *Come in. Come deeper. You're safe down here. . . .*

She didn't want to wall off the tunnel. She wanted to explore it.

She listened for a second, to make certain that no one was coming. Then she took another step down the tunnel. And another and another. Concentrating on the feel of the air and the soft sound of her feet on the bare earth. Her mind picked up sounds and smells, sorting them into the complex, intricate patterns they made and building a model of the space around her.

Now she could tell that there was more than one tunnel. More than two. She clicked her tongue against the roof of her mouth and heard the sound go off in all directions. Where did the tunnels lead? How many were there? . . .

She couldn't untangle the pattern without moving farther in. Something strange and familiar tugged at her mind, and she took another step. . . .

Patterns in the dark . . . Three and four and five.
More . . .
Over, under, over, over, under.
Flat and round and square . . .
Each one different . . .

It wasn't a picture in her mind and it wasn't a voice. But there was something. . . . if only she could catch hold of it. . . . Some sharp, inexplicable impression. She reached out toward it—

—and then Bando called from the ramp.

"Lorn! Lorn! Dess and Ab are coming—with lots of stones! We can start the wall now!"

Lorn's mind came floating back from somewhere far away. *I don't want to build a wall. I want to keep the way open and explore.* But she couldn't do that. The others wouldn't let her, and she'd never be able to persuade them.

"Lorn! Are you there?"

She turned quickly and walked back through the hole, shouting an answer to Bando. "Yes, I'm here. Bring the stones across and we'll get going!"

SHE MEANT TO BUILD A PROPER, SOLID WALL. ONE THAT blocked the hole completely. And she would have done it— if Bando hadn't started by making a mistake.

He came across from the ramp with two big stones in his arms. Even he was staggering under their weight, and when Lorn told him to put them down, he dropped them so quickly that she had to jump backward to avoid them.

"Be careful!" she said. "You nearly squashed my toes."

She didn't speak sharply, but Bando was horrified. "Did I hurt you? I didn't mean to hurt you, Lorn! I'm very, very sorry. Are you all right?"

He was still apologizing when Shang shouted from the ramp, with the next load of stones. Lorn sent Bando straight off to fetch them, to get him thinking about something else.

It was only when he'd gone that she realized there was a space between the two stones he'd dropped.

Quite a big space. Big enough for me to crawl through. . . .

The thought was there before she could stop it, shocking and enticing. She tried to blot it out, but she was too late. The idea had formed in her mind. If she left the stones where they were, she could make a secret passage through the wall.

It wouldn't be right, of course. It would mean deceiving the others. She couldn't possibly do it.

But if she did, no one would ever know. Bando would put the rest of the stones exactly where she told him, without asking questions. And by the time the others came down to look at the wall, the opening could be hidden behind a loose stone. Everyone would feel safe—and she would be free to explore the tunnels whenever she wanted to.

But she couldn't do it. Of course she couldn't. . . .

SHE REALLY DIDN'T MEAN TO MAKE A SECRET PASSAGE. But somehow she found herself leaving that tempting space exactly as it was. Every time Bando brought more stones, she guided him toward the other end of the wall—until it was almost as tall as she was, and she knew that she would have to level it off soon.

And then Bando picked another stone off the ramp—and called out gleefully, "This one's *huge*!"

His voice echoed off the stone, and it threw a long, dark shadow behind him as he hoisted it onto his shoulder. Lorn felt the shape of that stone inside her head, as though she'd already touched it. It was wide and flat and very long.

Long enough to bridge the gap between the other two stones.

Quickly and quietly, she moved along the wall, back to the low end. "Bring it this way," she called back. "Over here."

Bando blundered through the darkness, breathing heavily under the weight of the stone. When he reached her, Lorn slid her fingers around his huge hands and guided them into the right position.

"Put it here. That's right. On top of these two."

Bando hesitated. "It feels as though there's a gap," he said doubtfully.

"Don't worry about that." Lorn loosened his fingers so that the stone dropped into place. "It's not very big. We can fill it up with small stuff later on."

That was all it took. He went for the next load of stones without asking any more questions, and Lorn knew that he would forget all about it in a couple of minutes.

As soon as he'd gone, she knelt down and slid her hands into the space between the stones. Her fingers spread out to fit it, instinctively, as if they knew the shape. *Yes,* she thought. *That's how it should be.* It was exactly the right width. All she needed to do was scrape down a little way into the earth, to make it deeper. She worked at the soil between the stones, her hands moving confidently as she scooped it out.

By the time Bando came back with the next lot of stones, she had finished. She stood up and talked him across the storeroom, not thinking about what she'd just been doing. Her mind moved on, planning how to use the next lot of stones—and the next and the next and the next—to make a strong, impenetrable wall. A barrier that nothing could cross.

Except the person who knew about the secret passage winding through it, like the hidden strand of hair in a twelve-strand braid. The strand that was almost invisible, unless your fingers knew how to find it in the dark. . . .

11

"Open the bag!" Robert said, calling to Tom as he ran back across the parking lot. "There might be an address inside."

Tom pulled the zipper open, but he wasn't quick enough for Robert. Before he had a chance to look in the bag, it was wrenched away from him. Robert knelt down and dumped it on the ground, rummaging through it with both hands.

There wasn't much to look at. But on the bottom—under a neatly folded raincoat and three glossy computer magazines—was an empty wallet, with a name and address card in the plastic pocket inside.

Robert pulled it out and sat back on his heels. "Warren Armstrong," he said. Experimentally.

Tom looked over his shoulder. "Is that the right surname? For Lorn?"

"How would I know?" Robert shrugged. "People have different names in the cavern."

He said it as though it should have been obvious. Tom was irritated. "*Why* do they have different names?"

"Because they *are* different," Robert said impatiently. "Because it's not allowed to remember what happened before. Because—oh, what does it matter?" He frowned down at the card he was holding. "Where's Charrington Close?"

Tom shrugged. "Search me."

"I'd better find a street map." Robert scrambled up and slung the bag over his shoulder.

"You're not *going* there?" Tom said. "What about that man?"

"He's only a *man*. I'm not going to be afraid of him, am I? Not after facing a hedge-tiger."

What's a hedge-tiger? Tom thought. But he didn't bother to ask. He'd only get another annoying non-answer.

"Men can be dangerous, too," Tom said. "That man is—" But he couldn't explain the feeling he had about him. He wasn't dangerous like a wild animal, all teeth and claws. It was a different kind of danger. Weird and disturbing.

Robert wasn't listening, anyway. He'd already set off back to the square. By the time Tom caught up, he was in the bookshop, poring over a street map of the city.

Tom peered down at the page, trying to read the names upside down. "Have you found it?"

"It's somewhere in this part of the map." Robert pointed without looking up. "One of the little streets in this development up here."

Tom found it first. It was right at the top of the page, on the edge of the city. Directly under the double blue line that showed where the highway ran. He reached over and put his finger on it. "Must be noisy up there."

"Good for buses, though. There's bound to be one that goes up there. It's a really big development." Robert put the book back on the shelf and headed for the door. He was almost through it before he looked back for Tom. "You coming, Tosh?"

No, Tom wanted to say. *Not there.* But he didn't. He nodded and followed Robert down the hill to the bus station.

The bus took the main road going north out of the city. It plunged downhill and then up again, and on the right, the development ran all the way up to the highway embankment. Tom could see the cheap little houses laid out on the slope ahead. It was just starting to get dark, and the streetlamps came on as he watched, marking out a maze of twisting, interconnected roads.

Just before the highway, the bus swung across the road, turning right into the development. Robert put his face against the window, counting the left turns as they passed them. When they reached the third one, he stood up and rang the bell, grabbing Tom's arm with one hand and the sports bag with the other.

"That's it. Come on."

They jumped off the bus as soon as it reached the next stop and headed back to the little dead-end street. It was very short, with half a dozen houses on each side and an odd one squeezed in at the end. The extra house had an awkward, uncomfortable look, as though it had been crammed into a leftover plot of land. It faced straight down the street, blocking off the end, and the highway embankment loomed close behind it, topped by high fences to close off the traffic.

Tall cypress hedges ran down each side of the little front garden, continuing past the house and on into the back, and the house sat in a dark gap between two streetlamps. All its curtains were drawn, and there was only one dim light showing, in the window over the front door.

"Bet that's the house," said Tom.

"You're only guessing," Robert said.

He began to walk down the street, stopping at each house to check its number. But he needn't have bothered. Tom was right. When they'd counted carefully, all down the road, number fourteen turned out to be the odd house at the end.

"I'll knock on the door," Robert said. "And pretend I found the bag, lying around somewhere. You'd better keep out of sight, in case he recognizes you." He marched up the path and rang the doorbell.

Tom stepped back, so that the cypress hedge on the left of the garden shielded him. Now that it was almost dark, the hedge hid him completely, but he could peer through the branches and see the house, with Robert at the front door.

Behind the blank, curtained windows, everything was very still. Robert rang the bell again. Tom saw a sudden brightness as one of the upstairs curtains twitched. Then the front door opened.

It was the man. He didn't say anything. He just stood in the doorway, waiting.

Robert cleared his throat. "Mr. Armstrong?"

The man bent his head, acknowledging the name.

Robert held out the sports bag. Tom couldn't quite catch what Robert said, but he was obviously explaining how he'd found it. Whatever he said, it didn't make any visible impression on Mr. Armstrong. He stood there, listening impassively, and then held out his hand for the bag. It looked as if he might take it and shut the door in Robert's face without saying anything at all.

But Robert wasn't going to be put off so easily. "There's

84

one other thing," he said, raising his voice and keeping a tight hold on the bag. "Can you tell me—?"

The man in the doorway stiffened and drew back. It was only a slight movement. Robert probably hadn't noticed it at all. But Tom saw it, watching from behind the hedge. Mr. Armstrong looked . . . offended.

"It's not anything important," Robert said in a false, cheerful voice. "It's just that I couldn't help noticing this plait, and I wondered how it was made. I'm really interested in crafts like that, but I can't figure it out."

Mr. Armstrong's eyes narrowed, and he spoke for the first time, opening his mouth just wide enough to let out the words. "I don't know anything about it."

Robert tried again. "I know it's not important. But I'd love to find out about it. Who made it? Was it your daughter?"

"I haven't got a daughter," Mr. Armstrong said. His voice and his face were completely expressionless. "But I have got work to do. Thank you for bringing this back."

His hand shot toward the bag. He snatched it out of Robert's hands and shut the door in his face. For a second, Robert was obviously too startled to react at all. Then he reached up and rang the doorbell again.

Nothing happened.

He rang again, holding his thumb on the bell. After a few seconds, the door flew open again, and Mr. Armstrong reappeared.

"There's no reward," he said coldly. "Now go away. If I see you again, I shall have to call the police. Good night."

The door shut again, and Robert trailed back down the

path looking angry and frustrated. Tom came out from behind the hedge to meet him.

"I told you he was a horrible man," he said.

Robert nodded thoughtfully. "Why did he react like that? Was it because I asked him about his daughter?"

"Maybe he did have a daughter," Tom said. "And she died. Maybe his marriage split up, and he doesn't get to see her anymore. Or maybe he's never had one, and he just didn't want to talk to you—because he's a horrible man. You're not going to find out, Robbo. He'll never tell you anything."

"Then I'll have to find out another way." Robert looked back at the house, over his shoulder. Then he began to walk back down the road, toward the bus stop. "I'm sure there's something weird going on in that house."

"You can't do anything about it," Tom said. "He's not exactly going to let you in, is he?"

"I'll go around the back," Robert said doggedly.

"You can't. Didn't you see the fence at the side? I bet he keeps that gate bolted."

"I'm not going to use the *gate*."

"But there isn't another entrance."

"Yes, there is." Robert sounded almost as scornful as Emma. "I'll go in along the highway embankment."

12

"You're going *along the highway embankment?*" Emma said. "What good will that do?"

Robert ignored her. He had the street map spread out on the floor, and he was bent over it, studying the pattern of the streets.

"This is the way to get in," he said suddenly. "From this business park on the other side of the development. It looks as if there's a piece of open ground between the offices and the houses."

For a second, Tom thought Emma was going to explode. "That's *how*," she said. "Not *why*. I want to know the point of all this scrambling about. You don't really imagine you're going to find Lorn, do you? And even if you do find her, she won't know anything about you, or the cavern, or the other people in it. Not if she's anything like you were."

"You don't get it, do you?" Robert said without looking up. "You really don't get it."

"Of course she doesn't!" Tom said stoutly. "Because there isn't a reason. Except that you don't know when to give up." There was something surreal about agreeing with Emma, but he had to. Because she was right. "You're being ridiculous."

"Look." Robert sat back on his heels and took a long breath. "I saw one of my friends die. Then I lost the rest of them—after we'd been through all kinds of danger together.

After they'd saved me from dying. If there's anything that can help me understand why I went through all that, of course I want to find it. Wouldn't you?"

He said it fiercely, with such intensity that Tom didn't know how to reply. What he had said suddenly sounded very stupid to him.

"I guess I would," he mumbled.

Emma was watching Robert. "It's Lorn, too, isn't it?" she said. "You want to find her."

"Yes," Robert said. He looked down quickly at the map, and there was an awkward little silence.

"So how does it help if you climb along the highway embankment?" Emma said at last.

Robert shook his head. "I don't know. But I've got to do something—and I can't think of anything else. If you don't like it, leave me to do it on my own. No one's asking you to get involved." He went on scanning the street map.

Tom waited for Emma to argue. That was what she usually did. If she didn't get her own way the first time, she kept nagging away until Robert finally gave in. Not this time, though. She looked at Robert's bent head for a moment and gave a grudging nod. Then she glanced at Tom.

"Don't let him go on his own," she muttered.

Go with him yourself, Tom would have said a week ago. *If you're that bothered. I'm not taking orders from you.* But she wasn't giving orders now. She was . . . asking him for something. He met her eyes and found himself smiling at her.

"Don't worry. I'll make sure he's OK."

——

IT WAS TOTALLY DARK BY THE TIME THEY LEFT THE HOUSE. Tom had borrowed Emma's bike, and he and Robert cycled across the city to the north side. But they didn't follow the bus route. Instead, they took a narrow road that ran up the back of the housing development and stopped dead when it reached the highway.

Robert had been right about the open ground. It was a bit of wasteland at the back of the business park. They padlocked their bikes together and hid them under some bushes.

The highway embankment ran in a straight line behind the business park, across the end of the waste ground and past the back of the housing development. There was a fence along the bottom, but it looked battered and overgrown.

"No one's going to notice us unless we crash about," Robert said. "Let's go."

He began to move quickly and quietly over the scrubby ground, keeping to the shadows. Tracking games had always been a nightmare when Robert was involved. Tom could think of dozens of times when he'd given their team away by stumbling around in the bushes. But now he moved like a commando, silent and almost invisible. As if it mattered.

Nightbirds, Tom thought before he could stop himself. *Hungry monsters out hunting.* Watching Robert, he could suddenly imagine what it must be like to be in real physical danger. To look up and see a dark, predatory shape looming over you, blotting out the sky.

"Are you coming?" Robert called softly from somewhere ahead.

Tom set out after him, horribly aware of the sound of his own movements. He didn't catch up until he reached the embankment. Robert was on the other side of the fence, looking up at the steep, dark slope, and he gave Tom a hand to help him scramble over. High above them, the traffic was thundering by, but the steady *swoosh-swoosh-swoosh* seemed remote and unreal, like a noise from another planet. Reality was the dark slope where they stood, thick with brambles and small bushes.

Tom peered into the undergrowth. "We'll never get through that."

"Yes, we will," Robert said easily. "There'll be animal tracks through the bushes. And I've brought some clippers in case we get stuck. Come on." He went down on to all fours and began to crawl forward.

The ground was even wetter than Tom had expected, and he made a small, disgusted noise.

"Shhh," Robert hissed. "Once we're past that lane, we'll be beside people's gardens all the way. Keep your mouth shut and follow me."

Then he was off, without giving Tom time to reply.

IF THEY'D WALKED ALONG THE ROADS, THEY COULD HAVE reached the house in ten or fifteen minutes. But the journey along the embankment took well over an hour.

They might as well have been a million miles away from the houses they were passing. Tom found himself totally focused on the faint scuffling, scuttling noises in the bushes around them. Or the rustle of dry leaves suddenly disturbed.

Once there was the gleam of a pair of yellow eyes, startlingly close.

"Cat," Robert said. With an edge of distaste that Tom didn't quite understand.

They stayed close to the cold ground, wriggling under thorny branches and huddling behind bushes, always stopping and starting. It took so much concentration that it was a shock when Robert suddenly pointed ahead. Tom looked up—and saw a line of gardens running at right angles to the highway. It took him a moment to understand that they were looking at the back of the houses on one side of the Armstrongs' street.

The Armstrongs' house was almost completely hidden behind one of the cypress hedges. The sharp point of its roof was just visible, sideways on, rising above the feathery tops of the trees. Tom hadn't realized that the hedge went all the way around the house.

Why? The embankment would have cut out enough light on its own. Why would anyone decide to plant a tall, thick cypress hedge as well?

There was no chance to ask Robert. He was off again, working his way higher up the embankment, toward the fence at the top. Reluctantly, Tom followed him, digging his fingers into the loose earth. When they reached the top, they huddled against the barrier. It was cold and noisy and uncomfortable up there, and they had to hang on to the bushes to stop themselves from sliding down again.

"Why are we up here?" Tom whispered. "I thought you wanted—"

"Quiet!" Robert said sharply. "Look down there."

Tom turned around and understood. They had climbed above the level of the cypress hedge, and now they could see down into the garden. It was very small, but it wasn't the dark space that Tom expected to see. It was full of a cold, eerie light that showed up the tiny patch of grass. And the single tree. And the big, ugly rock garden.

There was nothing else. Most of the space was taken up by a hexagonal conservatory that jutted out from the back of the house. That was full of the same bleak, thin light as the garden. From where he was crouching, Tom could see straight down through the glass roof to a television, which was the source of the light.

It was facing out into the garden, and it was switched on, even though there was no one there to watch it. The lighted screen dominated the conservatory. The television was in the middle of the floor, on a bright red mat with a pattern of white tulips around the edge.

There was no other furniture, except a small table and a wooden kitchen chair. Both of them stood behind the television, next to the French windows that led into the house.

So where did you sit if you wanted to watch TV? Tom was trying to figure that out when Mr. Armstrong walked through the French windows and into the conservatory. Without even glancing at the television, he began to move heavily around the conservatory, pulling down blinds.

Every pane had its own separate blind, and he pulled them methodically, in a steady, regular rhythm, as though he did the same thing every day. As he covered the windows, one by one, the garden grew gradually darker. Looking down through the glass roof, Tom saw Mr. Armstrong switch on a light and then clamber onto the chair, reaching for the cords that operated the overhead blinds.

His head was turned up toward Tom, but he was talking over his shoulder to someone inside the house. As he pulled at the last blind, a thin, slight woman walked through the French windows into the conservatory. She stepped carefully over the threshold, concentrating on the loaded tray that she was carrying. Tom had a vague impression of dishes of food and bright primary colors.

The woman put the tray down on the table. She looked up to speak to Mr. Armstrong—and the final blind snapped down.

Tom let out his breath in a long, slow sigh.

"What did you make of all that?" he said.

There was no answer. Robert was right beside him, crouched under the same bush, but he didn't reply.

"Robbo?" Tom put out a hand and touched his arm. "What's up? Are you OK?"

"That woman—" Robert said. He sounded as though he could hardly get the words out.

"What about her?" Tom leaned closer, trying to make out his expression in the darkness. "What's the matter?"

"Her face—" Robert shook his head from side to side. "She—that's how Lorn looks. Not nearly as old as that but—it's the same face."

He's imagining it, Tom thought before he could stop himself. But he didn't say it out loud. He said, "Do you think it's her mother?"

"I don't know!" Robert said wildly. "How do I know it's not Lorn? Herself."

"Isn't she too old—?"

"I don't *know*." Robert's voice was savage. Desperate. "I don't know how any of it works. But I've got to go down there and talk to her."

"No!"

Tom grabbed at his arm, trying to hold him back. But he wasn't strong enough. Robert wrenched himself free and plunged down the embankment, toward the cypress hedge.

13

THE WALL WENT UP MUCH FASTER THAN LORN COULD ever have imagined. She'd been expecting to spend a lot of time on her own with Bando, waiting about for stones, but she found herself struggling to keep up.

The others were desperate to get the hole sealed. They toiled back and forth collecting stones all day and all night, not taking any rest until they were too cold to move or too exhausted to carry anything. And whenever anyone appeared at the top of the ramp, Lorn heard the same anxious questions.

"How high is it now? How much longer before it's finished?"

She always gave the same answer. "Not long. Just keep the stones coming." But it got harder and harder to sound cheerful. She and Bando were lifting heavy stones, with their hands held up in the air, and even though Bando was taking most of the weight, her muscles ached almost too much to move.

She managed to keep going until the wall was head high. Then Bando slid in a long, wide stone, and when she reached up to check how it had settled, an agonizing pain shot up her arm. She gasped, before she could stop herself.

"What's the matter?" Bando said quickly. "Are you hurt? Did I squash your fingers?"

It was a moment before Lorn could catch her breath.

When she managed to speak, she said, "Only tired . . . but . . . I can't keep going. Tell the others . . . they'll have to . . . help out."

"I'll get them!" Bando said. "Don't worry. I'll get them right away." He stumbled off across the storeroom, calling as he went. "You've got to come and help, or we can't finish the wall. Lorn says you've got to help."

Even he was tired now. Lorn could hear his feet dragging, and his voice sounded thin and tired. But he didn't have to shout for long. Almost immediately, people came running down the ramp.

"Stones," Lorn said feebly. "You need *stones*."

She hardly had the energy to raise her voice, but that didn't matter. As soon as Perdew realized what she was asking, he organized the others into a chain, passing stones from hand to hand, all the way across the storeroom.

There was no talking or laughter. They just worked as fast as they could, completely focused on getting the stones into place. No one made a sound for almost half an hour—until Bando jammed in the very last stone, on top of the center of the wall. They all heard it grating as it went into place.

"That's it," Lorn said. "It's finished."

There was an instant of silence—as if no one could quite believe it—and then Dess gave a great whoop of laughter. He came running across the space and thumped the wall as hard as he could.

"Look!" he shouted. "It's solid! We've done it! We're *absolutely safe*."

Annet gave a loud yell of delight. "Nothing can shift it!"

"Not ten elephants!" called Ab.

"Not twenty bulldozers." That was Shang.

"Not two blue whales!"

"Five tornadoes!"

"Ten tons of high explosive!"

They were silly with relief and exhaustion. Tina started giggling wildly, and Ab and Shang were pushing each other around. Lorn knew they were looking for a way to celebrate. It had been hard work, but they'd done it, and now they were all jammed into the storeroom together, and the air was alive with the warmth of their bodies and the smell of their sweat. They needed . . . they needed . . .

I can't do it for them, she thought. *I don't feel like that. . . .*

But she knew it didn't matter how she felt. She made herself open her mind and spread her hands—and the power came to her, as it always did, out of nowhere. Her exhaustion disappeared, and she knew, without thinking, what she had to do.

She began to smack her left hand against the palm of her right in a steady rhythm, just slower than her heartbeat. At first, she could hardly hear it herself against the buzz of voices around her. But she kept the noise going, and gradually, the others stopped talking and turned toward her in the dark.

As they turned, she began to move, shifting from foot to foot in a way that was not quite marching and not quite dancing. No one could see what she was doing, but the people nearest to her felt it, and they squeezed out of her way. Turning her back on the new wall, she began to travel forward, toward the ramp.

The others shuffled aside, opening up a path. As she

moved down it, they began tapping out the rhythm she was beating. They fell into step behind her, and she led them up the ramp and out into the light, slipping past the brazier and into the main cavern.

It was crowded and congested, with every spare inch full of stored food, and floss for weaving, and fur blankets folded up together. Lorn wove a path between the heaps, and the dancers followed her, in a line that grew longer and longer as they came up out of the storeroom.

When they were all up, she led them into a great trampling circle in front of the brazier. Gradually her steps grew smaller, until she was moving on the spot. Then she turned in, toward the center of the circle, and made herself tread faster and faster, beating the ground with her feet.

Faster and faster, keeping time with her hands, clapping and stamping until all the others were copying her and the whole cavern was full of noise and movement.

Faster and faster and faster and faster, until they couldn't accelerate anymore. Until the movement and the speed and the noise were almost too much to bear—and she had to resolve the whole thing into a single great shout.

"We did it!"

She threw up her hands and yelled, and the others copied her, shouting as loudly as they could.

"WE DID IT!"

And then they were all laughing. All except Lorn. The crowd broke up into small groups of chattering, excited people. It had been a massive, exhausting effort, but they'd built the wall, and the storeroom was safe, sealed off from the darkness on the other side.

"We need to eat," Tina said. "We're all starving."

Lorn nodded. "Get them to sit down, and then give out double shares of everything. We'll have a feast."

There was a huge cheer and more laughter. But as people began to sit down, Lorn stood off to one side, struggling to smile. Even that felt false and forced. The others were celebrating because the tunnels had been shut off—and she knew that wasn't true.

She'd deceived them all.

When the feast was over, people lay back sleepily, talking to each other and glancing surreptitiously at Lorn. She knew what they were waiting for. After a meal like that, Zak would have taken out his drum. Softly at first, and then louder and louder, he would have beaten out a rhythm with his fingers, letting it swell until every face turned toward him.

And then he would have put the drum down and begun to speak, starting out on a story. He always knew the right story for the moment. That was his job. Knowing how they felt and what they wanted—even when they didn't know it themselves.

It had been Zak's job—and now it was Lorn's. She didn't understand how the power had come to her, but ever since Zak went traveling she had found herself with the right words for whatever the others needed. She could start the story that came to her without worrying about how it would end. Because the end was always right.

That was what they wanted now. But tonight, all she had in her head was a single word. It was painful and unwelcome, not suited to a celebration, and she fought to hold it back. For as long as she could, she kept her head bent, playing with the braid that lay in her lap.

But it was no use. They were all looking toward her, and in the end, the pressure was too strong to resist. She lifted her head and spoke the word out loud.

"Cold."

It silenced everyone, faster than Zak's drumbeat ever had. The cavern was instantly still, with no sound except the shifting of logs on the fire. Lorn breathed in, letting the stillness flow into her, like an icy liquid pouring into her body. As she drew it in, more words welled up in her mind.

"The cold is coming now," she said. "It's coming fast for us, but it will come even faster for people above the ground—for people who are traveling."

Annet gasped. The noise sounded raw and harsh in the silence, but Lorn went on relentlessly.

"Travelers set out full of hope and excitement. They want to reach impossible places. They want to change the way things are."

She didn't need to say the names—*Cam* and *Zak*, *Robert* and *Nate*. Everyone knew whom she meant. She could feel them making pictures in their heads as she went on.

"They carry heavy packs of food," she said. "And thick furs, to keep out the cold. At night they huddle together, burrowing deep into dead leaves, with the furs wrapped close around them. With every breath and every step they take, they fight against the cold, struggling to reach home. But the journey seems unending. Every day they grow weaker. And the cold grows stronger."

"They need a rescue," Bando said, not interrupting in his normal loud voice, but whispering the words, his face tight with concentration.

Lorn shook her head, spreading out her hands. "Who can rescue them? They're lost in the great wide spaces above ground. Each day it grows colder and colder. And soon the frosts will come."

She saw the white frost crystals, clear and sharp in her mind, and the travelers' breath, hanging in the air like drops of water. She felt how their bodies slowed as their blood grew sluggish and thick.

The fire crackled and spat.

The story was like a weight. Its dark words blocked Lorn's throat, and she didn't know what end to give it except the harsh, bleak truth that all of them knew instinctively. And feared. And ignored.

It was already very cold. Even inside the cavern, the temperature was lower every day. What did it matter whether they built walls or not? The end would be the same, whatever they did. It was going to get colder and colder, until they all died.

First—very soon—it would be the travelers. Cam and Zak and Nate and Robert would never come back. They would all die out there in the cold, twisted into stiff, hungry shapes on the frozen ground.

And then, one by one, the same thing would happen to the rest of them. Robert had gone to find a way of saving them, but he would never come back now. And soon, even the thickest fur would be too thin to keep them warm. One by one, they would go to sleep and never wake again. For the first time, Lorn understood that clearly. That was how the story was bound to end. It was the way things were.

But when she lifted her head and looked at the earnest faces watching her, she knew they weren't waiting for that kind of ending. They were watching her lips as though her words could change the future. As though telling the story could alter what had to happen.

Her mind was empty of everything except despair, but those faces drew her up onto her feet and sent her walking across the cavern. She went between the bundles and around the heaps of grain until she reached the journey line.

Once, there had been four stones lying on that line. Now there were only two. Nate's black stone was lost, and Robert's yellow one was where she had pushed it, deep down into the earth. The other two were cold and heavy in her hand as she picked them up and walked back to her place.

"Stoke up the brazier," she said.

Everyone was too startled to move, but she said it again. Louder this time, so that her voice resounded from end to end in the cavern.

"Stoke up the brazier! Bring more wood! These stones are cold and we need to make them warm!"

She held them out on her open palm for everyone to see. Ab was on duty by the woodpile, and he looked nervously at her, over his shoulder. She gave him an impatient nod.

"There's no time to waste! We need the biggest fire you can make. Pile on the wood."

Ab bent down and heaved up two logs, lifting them high so that Tina could reach them from the stoker's ledge.

"More!" Lorn said sharply. She waved an arm at the

others. "Ab and Tina can't do it fast enough on their own! Help them!"

They hesitated for a moment, obviously bewildered. Then they responded to the authority in her voice, scrambling up and converging on the woodpile. Suddenly they were handing up logs so fast that Tina couldn't deal with them. Ab hauled himself up beside her, and the two of them worked together, heaping the logs into the fire until there was a great red mound, way above the rim of the brazier.

Perdew was the only one who didn't join the rush. He stood at Lorn's elbow, watching as the others worked and the heat grew stronger. A lurid red light filled the whole cavern, and the air was hot and foul with smoke.

"What are you up to, Lorn?" he said softly.

Lorn's fingers closed tight around the two stones in her hand. "We have to do this," she said, not taking her eyes off the brazier.

Perdew shook his head. "It's taking too much wood. We can't afford to use so much."

"There'll be more wood." Lorn heard the confidence in her own voice and wondered where it came from. The top layer of the woodpile was almost used up now, and the smoke that was billowing around the cavern was too thick for their small smoke-hole to clear. She could smell charring as the shooting flames licked at the roots that looped across the roof.

"The air's going bad!" Perdew pulled at her arm, raising his voice to make sure she could hear him above the roaring of the fire and the hubbub around the brazier. "What are you trying to do? Smother us all to death?"

Lorn didn't even look at him. She was leaning forward, staring into the flames. "We have to do this," she said stubbornly. "We must defeat the cold."

Her lungs were so tight that she could hardly breathe, but she kept them piling on the wood, watching the fire burn higher and higher until the metal of the brazier itself began to glow dull red. It was impossible for anyone to stay close to it. Through the smoke, she saw Ab and Tina slide off the stoking ledge. They backed away, and one by one the others followed them, staring in silence as the bright logs settled and sparked.

Once they stopped stoking, the brightness faded quickly. A dull gray bloom crept across the glowing metal. After a while, Tina and Ab picked up the long rods that they used to riddle the fire. Moving together, they pushed them into the lowest holes in the brazier, and slid them backward and forward, clearing the ash. The logs settled noisily, subsiding below the rim of the brazier.

Everywhere the smoke hung thick and choking. Lorn was too tired to speak. When Bando came to take the stones out of her hand, she let him open her fingers, almost without registering what he was doing.

Then Perdew took her arm and led her to the place where she slept, bundling one of her fur blankets into a pillow. She slept instantly, exhausted, as though she had spent the whole day struggling over rough ground.

14

ROBERT VANISHED INTO THE DARKNESS, MOVING QUIETLY and fast. After a second or two, Tom couldn't even hear him crawling through the undergrowth. There was no sound except the hum of the traffic from behind and the blare of the television below.

Tom wanted to keep out of it, but he couldn't. Not when he could see Robert heading straight for trouble. He was waiting for it all to make sense, but it didn't. Why was Robert so set on finding this girl? And how had he learned to move like that?

Tom found himself inching down the embankment, too. At first he tried to find some sort of track, a way through that showed where Robert had been. But there didn't seem to be any break in the undergrowth. Brambles snagged his clothes and branches whipped across his legs. Twice, he put his hand straight into a lump of thistles, and once, a long nettle wrapped itself agonizingly around his face. He kept struggling on but couldn't see anything clearly through the darkness. Not until he was almost level with the top of the cypress hedge.

Then everything changed suddenly. Luridly.

High on the back wall of the house, a security lamp erupted into life, and the whole garden was caught in its ugly glare. The harsh white light was thrown up the embankment, too, and all at once the darkness seemed more like a friend than an enemy. Tom slid down another foot or so, into the shadow of the hedge.

Robert wasn't so lucky. He was halfway across the grass, on all fours, when the white glare caught him, crawling between the hedge and the conservatory. He was totally exposed.

There was no time to stand up and run. Before he could move at all, the conservatory door flew open and a bulky figure shot out, heading straight toward him. Peering through the hedge, Tom saw Mr. Armstrong fling himself at Robert, pinning him to the ground.

There was a brief struggle. Tom thought Robert might break away, but Mr. Armstrong was twice Robert's weight, and very determined. It was only a few seconds before he grabbed Robert around the body and hauled him onto his feet. Spinning him around, he clamped an arm across his throat, from behind, dragging him backward and pulling him off balance.

Mr. Armstrong's thin, wet mouth was close to his ear, spitting words into it. Tom couldn't hear what he was saying, but it wasn't hard to guess. Every time he spoke, he gave Robert a vicious shake, for emphasis. Robert scrabbled at the arm around his throat, trying to stay on his feet and save himself from choking. But he couldn't pull it away.

Tom wanted to charge out of hiding and throw himself into the fight. But he was stranded up on the embankment, with a thick hedge in the way. All he could do was watch. He saw Robert's mouth move, forcing out a few words, but that just brought him another shaking. This time it was so fierce that his face twisted with pain.

Then Mr. Armstrong shouted, calling over his shoulder, toward the house. "Warren!"

For a second nothing happened, and he called again, irritably.

"Warren!"

The back door opened slowly, and Warren came sidling out of the kitchen. He peered warily into the garden, looking miserable and sullen.

His father said something in a lower voice, with an impatient jerk of his head. Tom couldn't make out the words, but he saw Warren dive back inside the house. When he came out again, he was carrying something.

Mr. Armstrong waved a hand at him, pointing and giving instructions, but Tom didn't guess what was going on. Not until Robert was hauled around to face the other way and Warren came in close, holding something out in front of him.

It was a camera. They were going to take a photograph.

Robert realized it, too, and he tried to turn away. But the man caught hold of his hair and pulled his head around to face the camera. Warren bobbed about, taking two or three pictures in quick succession. Then his father waved him away, nodding toward the gate at the side of the house. Obediently, Warren scuttled across to it and fumbled with the bolts.

By the time he got them open, Mr. Armstrong was there, too, dragging Robert along with him. He gave him a last shake and then shoved him through the gate. Robert staggered down the path, and Mr. Armstrong closed the gate quickly behind him, shooting the bolts back into place.

Warren disappeared into the house, but his father didn't follow him right away. He walked slowly down the garden, peering into the hedges on both sides. When he reached the far end, he stepped back and began to scan the embankment.

Tom knew he was well hidden. There was no reason to be afraid. But as the cold eyes came toward him, he found himself shivering and huddling lower into the brambles, feeling vulnerable and afraid. Terrifyingly aware of the eyes sliding over the trees that shielded him.

They reached the place where he was crouched—and stopped. For a long, appalling moment, Tom kept completely still, not even breathing. The man in front of him was a faceless shape, silhouetted in the glare of the security light. It was impossible to tell what he was thinking or what he could see.

Just when Tom thought his lungs were going to burst, the silhouette shifted, moving farther along the hedge. Tom lowered his head onto his hands and bit on his fingers to stop himself shaking.

A moment later, it was over. Mr. Armstrong turned around and went back into the conservatory, closing the door behind him and leaving the garden empty. After a little while, the security light went off and everything was dark again, except for the glow from the television, seeping out around the edges of the all-concealing blinds.

Tom stayed still for a long time, gazing down at those blinds. At first, he was simply watching for shadows behind them, trying to see what was going on inside. But gradually he began to think about the blinds themselves.

What was the point of pulling them in the dark? The gar-

den was hidden already, shut in by its tall hedges. Nobo[d]
could look into the conservatory without climbing along t[h]
embankment—and only an obsessive like Robert would [do]
that. Why was Mr. Armstrong going to so much trouble [to]
protect the conservatory?

What was going on in there?

From up on the slope, Tom could still hear the faint sou[nd]
of the television, and every now and again, he could see [a]
blurred shape dancing over the drawn blinds. But that w[as]
all. If he wanted to find out anything else, he would have [to]
get closer.

He studied the position of the security lamp. Robert h[ad]
walked straight into that trap and set it off. But suppose he[']
taken a different route? Suppose he'd stayed in the hed[ge]
and crawled around the edge of the garden to the left-ha[nd]
side? Over there, the conservatory was close to the hedge. [It]
masked that part of the garden from the security light.

It wouldn't be very difficult to get around there. . . .

Tom began to move cautiously down the slope, feeling h[is]
way with both hands and keeping a close watch on the co[n]-
servatory. When he reached the bottom, he found hims[elf]
facing a strong wooden fence running along between hi[m]
and the hedge.

He hadn't expected that, but it just made him more dete[r]-
mined—because it was another way of keeping people out [of]
the garden. He looked along the fence, searching for a pla[ce]
where the cypress branches hung down over it, low enoug[h]
to reach.

He had to stand on tiptoe to grab the branches when h[e]
found them, but once he had a secure grip, it was easy. H[e]

hauled on the branches, walking his feet up the fence, and scrambled into the tree on the other side.

It was tempting to stay up there, breathing in the clean, bitter smell of the cypress. He would have liked to travel around the garden that way, climbing from tree to tree, but the network of branches was too thick to penetrate. Reluctantly, he let himself down into the garden and started to move carefully from tree to tree, keeping back against the fence.

It seemed a long way to the corner. When he reached it, he turned down the left-hand side of the garden, toward the conservatory. It was much closer now. He could hear the sound from the television quite clearly, and underneath it, a faint mutter of voices.

There was something odd about the pattern of those voices. One deep voice (Mr. Armstrong's?) dominated the others, not speaking continuously but repeating the same phrases over and over. Occasionally, there was an answer in a higher voice, and once or twice, Tom thought he heard a third one, very faint. He went on moving steadily toward the sounds, his feet silent on the soft silt of fallen cypress leaves.

It was hard to leave the shelter of the trees. When he finally drew level with the conservatory, he had to force himself to lie down and wriggle out onto the grass. It was cold and wet with dew, and he felt the water soaking into his clothes as he squirmed forward.

The conservatory had a solid brick base. He lay up against it, listening. The television sounded very close—nearer than he had expected—but there was no other sound that he could detect. Had everyone gone? He levered himself up

slowly, until he was high enough to peer over the top of the brickwork.

Like all the other windows, the window in front of him was covered by a thick blind. It fitted very well, but at the edge a narrow line of light was leaking out. Shutting one eye, Tom leaned forward to peer through the tiny gap.

All he could see was a solid, silvery surface. Something was pushed up against the other side of the glass, blocking his view. For a moment, he couldn't imagine what it was. Then a voice spoke out of it, clear and unmistakable.

"You'll need half a pound of cod fillet—"

It was the side of the television. For some reason, the television had been moved from the middle of the conservatory. No one had bothered to switch it off, even though it was jammed right up against the window.

Ducking down, Tom crawled a little way farther along, to the edge of the next blind. This time, when he raised his head, there was nothing to block his view. Peering around the side of the blind, he could see straight across the conservatory.

And what he saw made his mouth drop open.

15

THERE WAS A HOLE IN THE FLOOR OF THE CONSERVATORY, right in the very center. A great, black hole, completely square, going down into the earth.

The woman he and Robert had seen earlier was kneeling on the very edge of the hole, gripping the rim with both hands. She was bending forward to look down into it, and Tom could see that she was talking softly. The television masked the sound of what she was saying, but he could see her lips moving and her head tilting first one way and then another.

Mr. Armstrong came into view, standing opposite her on the other side of the hole. He didn't speak. He just stood there, staring. The woman shuffled back apologetically and scrambled onto her feet, wiping her hands on her skirt. As soon as she was out of the way, Mr. Armstrong looked down into the hole and said something short and sharp. Then he and the woman walked out of view for a moment. When they came back, they were carrying a big, square board with dozens of little perforations drilled through it. Together, they bent down and maneuvered it into position, fitting it over the hole like a lid. It dropped down into the opening, so that it lay level with the floor.

Moving automatically, without speaking, the woman fetched the red rug and unrolled it over the board, hiding it completely. She pulled the rug straight, very carefully, so that the white tulips marched down each side in neat, even rows. There was not even a wrinkle to hint at anything strange underneath.

Just in time, Tom realized that the television would be moved next. He dived down below the level of the windows and crouched very still, listening to the noise change as the television went back to its original position. It was a long time before he felt safe enough to raise his head again.

When he did, everything looked just as it had when he first gazed down into the conservatory. The television was in the middle, on the red tulip rug, throwing its pale, thin light onto the blinds at the end. Tom couldn't see anyone, and for a second, he thought the whole place was empty.

Then something moved, low down on the ground. He shifted slightly, changing his angle of vision, and saw a neat, small head, with brown hair pulled back tightly into a knot. It was the woman. She was on her knees, with her back to him, polishing the conservatory floor. Tom couldn't see any marks on it, but she kept moving briskly, rubbing hard at the wooden boards with the cloth she was holding.

Then she began on the legs of the table and the seat of the rough, old kitchen chair, rubbing and rubbing at stains too small for Tom to make out. Gradually she turned around, and he saw her face, tense with concentration. Her lips were moving, and she kept muttering and frowning and ducking her head, just as she had when she was looking down into the hole.

Was she singing? Reciting poetry? Memorizing a shopping list? Tom tried to lip-read, but he couldn't make out a single word.

Then she stood up to start work on the tabletop, and her head disappeared out of Tom's field of vision. Cautiously, he stood up so that he could go on watching her. As he did, he saw that the tray she'd brought in was still there, lying on top of the table.

When she'd first brought it in, it hadn't seemed important. Tom had seen it through the roof of the conservatory, but he'd hardly glanced at it. Now everything on it seemed like a possible clue. There was a red plastic plate, like a dog's bowl, with a dirty spoon lying in it. In one corner was a dishcloth, and lying next to it was a pair of big, heavy scissors.

But—hadn't the bowl been full of food when she brought it in? It was empty now, but there were smears of green and brown all over the bottom and the sides. Hadn't the dishcloth been folded neatly? Now it was screwed up into a dirty ball. The rest of the tray was smeared too, as though someone had spread the contents of the bowl all over it, with both hands.

And there was at least one thing missing. Tom tried to remember what it was, but the image was elusive. His mind teased him with vague impressions of a tall, brightly colored shape that he couldn't identify. What *was* it?

He was concentrating so hard that he didn't hear the kitchen door open. So he was completely unprepared for the sudden glare of the security light and the pale, pudgy face that peered around the outside corner of the conservatory.

It was Warren.

He obviously wasn't expecting to see Tom. His eyes widened and he opened his mouth to yell. But as Tom looked up, their eyes met—and Warren recognized him. For one crucial second, he was too startled to make a sound.

Tom reacted instinctively, jumping up to face him. Darting his face forward, he hissed the first thing that came into his head. "Don't you mess with me! I know where you live, Warren Armstrong!"

The effect was out of all proportion. Warren's face went white and he shrank away, as if he was used to being bullied. Tom felt slightly sick, but he didn't waste his chance. Before Warren could recover, he raced for the cover of the cypress hedge.

There was no time to work his way along it and go back the way he'd come. He simply scrambled up the nearest tree and threw himself over the fence, into the garden next door. As he hit the ground, he heard Warren start to shout.

"Dad! Come here! *Dad!*"

The kitchen door opened again, and a cold voice said, "What is it? Be quiet!"

Tom didn't wait to hear any more. He flung himself down the garden where he had landed, heading for the far corner. There, at the farthest tip, the garden just touched the highway embankment. If he could get out onto the embankment, he would be safe. No one would be able to track him down in those tangled bushes. Not without a helicopter.

The fence at the corner of the garden was low and dilapidated, with a compost heap built up against it. It was easy to scramble over and crawl into the undergrowth. He managed it just in time. A few seconds later, he glimpsed a light coming down toward him, flicking first into one garden and then into the other. And as it came, a cold voice was calling. It wasn't loud, but it was the most frightening voice he'd ever heard.

"Come out and speak to us. Otherwise we shall call the police. You can't escape. Come out and talk."

Tom had no intention of talking to Mr. Armstrong. He lay as still as he could in the brambles at the bottom of the embankment, huddled close against the fence. Trying not to shiver as he listened to that cold, controlled voice. It had no expression in it at all. Not even a threat. But the more he listened to it, the more he wished Mr. Armstrong *would* call the police.

But he won't do it. Whatever he says. That was the threat he'd used to get rid of Robert before. *If I see you again, I shall have to call the police.* But he hadn't done it. Even though he'd found Robert in the garden, heading for his house. It would have been perfectly reasonable to call the police then. But all he'd done was take a stupid picture.

The voice called again, from farther along the hedge. "It's no use trying to hide. If you do, we'll get the police to find you."

Tom lay still and watched the flashlight going up and down the fence for almost a quarter of an hour, with the cold voice calling softly to him, alternately threatening and wheedling. Even when it stopped, he didn't come out of hiding. He lay where he was, while the security light went out and the garden settled into a dark, rustling silence.

When it had been empty and quiet for a long time, he began to crawl slowly through the bushes, heading back along the embankment. The brambles still tore at his clothes and scratched his face, but this time he barely felt them. His mind was going over and over the things he'd seen, trying to make sense of them. But he couldn't.

All he knew was that he had to get back and talk to Robert.

16

Lorn woke in the middle of the night. Cold air was blowing down through the entrance, turning her cheek numb and making her teeth ache. She sat up, rubbing at her face—and saw a cavern full of sleepers.

Dess and Bando were awake, because they were looking after the fire, but all the others were fast asleep, curled up under heaps of bat-fur blankets. The cavern was quiet except for the scrape of logs being moved.

I could go down to the storeroom now, Lorn thought. *I could go without being seen.*

It wasn't a conscious decision. As soon as the thought came to her, she was sliding out from under her furs, making for the shadows at the side of the cavern. Her bare feet were silent on the trampled earth, and no one stirred as she went by.

Even the stokers weren't a problem. It was easy to get past them without being seen. When Dess lifted a log over the rim of the brazier, Bando looked toward the fire, too, grinning in the red light. He loved watching the rush of sparks as the log fell into the flames.

In that moment, Lorn slipped quickly forward, past the brazier and into the shadowy place behind. Then, as Bando turned away to pick up a new log, she padded forward and down the ramp, moving silently on the soft earth.

When she reached the darkness beyond the ramp, she

closed her eyes and let her mind change gear. Her other senses stirred and took over, and she turned her head and sniffed at the swirling air, flaring her nostrils wide to catch the changing scents. As she sniffed, she shifted from one foot to the other, listening to the faint noise they made on the soft earth.

In a few seconds, she knew exactly where she was aiming. She could feel the wall on the other side of the space and taste the damp sourness of the earth that held it together. Walking quickly and surely across the storeroom, she knelt down in front of the wall. And her hands went straight to the hidden passage.

She had disguised it with two stones, one at each end, so that even with a light, no one else would be able to find it. But she knew exactly where it was. With one tug, she pulled the loose stone out of the wall, rolling it away to one side.

There was a quick trickle of earth and then silence. She could feel a draft of colder air coming through from the other end.

Quickly, before she could think about what might happen, she went head first into the hole, squirming through the narrow space on her stomach. Some of the earth had fallen and settled, leaving unexpected ridges and gaps. As she worked herself along, she updated the images in her mind so that she knew the shape of the passage exactly.

When she reached the stone that blocked the other end, she wriggled forward and laid her hands flat against it. Putting all her weight behind them, she pushed once, twice, three times.

The stone rolled out of the way, and she fell forward into the empty space beyond the wall.

THE MOMENT SHE WAS IN THE TUNNEL, SHE FELT A CHANGE in the air around her. It was much colder on that side of the wall—cold enough to make her shiver—and it smelled quite different. Back in the storeroom, the walls were drying out already, in the heat that came down the ramp. This tunnel had the damp scent of living earth. And another scent, too, rank and animal. She stood up and took a long breath, trying to recognize the smell, but she couldn't figure out what it was.

Then she put out a hand to touch the wall, and her knuckles brushed against soft, loosening earth. In the darkness, its texture against her skin was suddenly, shockingly familiar. Her mind flooded with—what?

Not memories, exactly. There were no pictures in her head, no sudden links with something in the past. It was more as though the damp smell and the loose earth . . . belonged to her. As though she knew them better than anything else in the world.

Everything drew her on, into the tunnel. *Go down*, said a voice inside her head. *If you want to be safe, if you want to understand, then you have to go down. . . .*

Clicking her tongue softly against the roof of her mouth, she turned her head to the right, letting the image of the tunnel sharpen in her head. It sloped slightly upward, and a faint draft of fresh, new air floated down toward her.

That way led to the surface, sooner or later.

When she turned the other way, the sounds and the smells were quite different. She could hear the tunnel going down into the earth, constantly twisting and turning, until her mind couldn't work out the shapes anymore. The air there was breathable, but the animal smell was much stronger.

She turned that way, shuffling soft earth under her feet as she moved forward. With every step she took, the close, meaty scent grew stronger, clinging to the walls. She couldn't help picturing the huge animal that had left the scent, pushing along the tunnel with its damp fur dragging against every surface. She imagined its head darting about and its hot, hungry eyes peering into the shadows while its nose sniffed greedily at the air.

Why take the risk of meeting a creature like that?

The rational part of her mind knew the danger she was running, but something stronger kept her moving on and down, putting one foot automatically in front of the other. After a few minutes, she came to a place where the tunnel forked into two, and she faced each branch in turn, speaking aloud to test how they sounded.

"I'm Lorn. I'm exploring."

The left-hand tunnel twisted away to the right, rising slightly as it went. The other one sloped downward, going deeper into the earth. She chose that one, not understanding why but stepping decisively into it. Going farther down.

She had walked about a hundred steps when she heard the first, faint noise.

It wasn't what she was expecting—and fearing. She'd been listening for scrabbling and scraping and the breathing of some big, warm-blooded animal. But what she heard was different.

It was a sticky, gliding, slithering sound, faint but unmistakable, coming from somewhere ahead. She could hear the suck and kiss of wet, ridged surfaces sliding against each other, in a pattern so complicated that she couldn't work it out.

What kind of shapes would make that noise? Her mind slid away from the effort of visualizing them, refusing to turn the sounds into pictures. But she knew—she *knew*—that she had heard those sounds before. She screwed up her eyes and began to hum, forcing herself to concentrate on the echoes that came back to her.

I know what that is. I know—

Her mind reached out, determined and insistent. At first, it met the usual blank barrier that shut out all her memories. But this time, she wouldn't accept the barrier. Everything was crying out to her now. The smell of the air, the feel of the earth, the slithering sounds deep under the ground.

I will remember. I WILL.

With all the force of her mind, she pushed at the barrier—and suddenly it broke. Images came pushing up from the darkness at the bottom of her mind, not separate and detached like pictures, but part of herself. As close as her own body.

And completely incomprehensible.

Noise is bad, noise from the mouth is bad, bad, bad. BAD GIRL. And the hair goes. They take the hair away. . . .
Over, over, under, over—no. No way to make the patterns anymore. Only the fingers turning and twisting and turning . . .
Only the hands going up and down the black room,

hunting, wanting, empty, empty . . .
Searching for anything to make the patterns.
And then finding the shapes. One, two, three . . .

Her hands remembered. Not giant slithering shapes, but small, small, small. From *before*. She knew exactly how they had felt between her fingers. How they'd slid away, refusing to keep the patterns. The memory was real. It was hers.

But her brain couldn't decipher it. Where had she been? And why had she been so desperate to twist those slithering, ungovernable shapes into neat, tight braids?

It didn't make *sense*. She struggled to grasp the images, but they slipped away from her explanations, refusing to be understood. Determination wasn't enough. She needed something more, another memory. . . .

It didn't come. Instead, a sound from outside broke in, forcing itself on her attention. Someone was calling her name, not very close, but nearer than any voice should have been.

"Lorn!"

For a moment, the word had no meaning for her. She was away in another place, feeling long, wet shapes slide through her fingers, and Lorn had nothing to do with her. She was . . . she was—

"Lorn! Where are you? LORN!"

It was Bando's voice. And as she recognized it, she realized why it sounded so close. He was down in the storeroom, very near the wall, and his shouts were coming straight through the secret passage. Because she'd left the entrance open.

Turning around, she began to run back the way she had come. He mustn't find that entrance. He mustn't come through. And she had to stop him shouting, before anyone else came down to see what was going on.

When she reached the rough stones of the new wall, she flung herself down onto her knees, going feet first into the passage. As soon as she was in, she pulled the loose stone after her, to seal the entrance. Then she wriggled backward as fast as she could, desperate to get through.

Speed made her careless. Once she was in the passage, she stopped listening and thinking, and all her energy went into moving. She had no idea why Bando was blundering around the storeroom in the dark, but as long as he was on his own, she was sure she could stop him from suspecting anything.

She hadn't counted on coming out right beside him.

He'd given up shouting. He was standing in the dark, leaning against the wall, and as she slid out of the passage, her legs brushed against his ankles. He yelped and bent down to push them away.

"Get off!" he said, sounding panicky and disgusted.

Then his fingers closed around her right ankle, and she felt him hesitate.

"It's all right, Bando," she hissed. "It's only me."

But it was too late. He'd found the entrance to the secret passage. She heard him catch his breath as he turned toward her, and his voice was shrill with panic.

"You've been through the wall, haven't you? *You've been in the tunnel!*"

17

By the time Tom got back to the place where they'd left their bikes, he was so tired that he could hardly stand. As he slid down the embankment, he didn't know how he was going to climb the rickety fence.

But Robert was there, waiting for him in the dark. Robert hauled him over onto the waste ground and guided him across it.

"Are you OK? I thought you were never coming. What happened?"

"I went down—I saw—" Tom couldn't dredge up the right words to explain. His exhausted brain refused to work. He wasn't even sure how much of what he'd seen was real and how much was imagination.

Robert gave him a careful look. "Save it," he said. "We can talk tomorrow. You need to concentrate on getting home while you can still cycle."

"But that house—"

"Tomorrow." Robert bent down and unlocked the bikes. "If we start talking now, we'll be out till midnight—and there'll be too many questions to answer. Come around tomorrow morning, and then we can try and make sense of it all."

For once, Tom was happy to be ordered around. He wobbled his way home, with Robert cycling carefully behind

him, and went to bed as soon as he got in—before his
mother had time to notice the state of his clothes.

Maybe it would all be clear and ordinary in the morning. He was just overreacting because he was so tired. There
had to be a simple explanation for what he'd seen. There had
to be.

"How do you know it was a secret room?" Emma
said. "And not just a hole under the floor?"

That was the question Tom had been asking himself
ever since he woke up. He'd been so sure, last night. But
what had he actually seen? Just a dark space with a trapdoor. It was probably the place where they kept their bar-
becue.

He shook his head. "It's not *what* I saw. It's the way they
covered it up, with the rug and the television. It's a pointless
place to put a television. And they seem desperate to keep
people out. There's a hedge *and* a fence *and* blinds *and* a security light."

Emma shrugged and sat back on her bed. "So maybe
they keep their money under the floor instead of putting
it in the bank. It's a nutty thing to do, but it's none of our
business."

"Except that Lorn's in there somewhere," Robert said.

Emma rolled her eyes. "Just because that woman looked
a bit like her?"

"She looks *exactly* like her. And there's the plait, as well."
Robert chewed at his lip. "It's weird, Em. You've got to
admit that."

"Maybe you're the one who's weird," Emma said. But it was a joke. Even Tom could tell that. She looked carefully at him. "Tell us again, Tom. Why are you so sure there's something strange about this hole under the floor?"

Tom didn't know where to start. There was the way Mr. Armstrong had driven Robert away. Twice. And there was the woman, with her scrubbing and talking to no one. And—

"There was a tray," he said slowly. He'd almost forgotten it until that moment, but now he could see it clearly in his mind. Bright, colored plastic, with food smeared across it.

"I saw that, too," Robert said. "It was just someone's supper."

"But you didn't see it afterward. All messed up with food." Tom shook his head. "Mr. Armstrong wouldn't have done that, would he? Nor would the woman. You ought to have seen how she cleaned up afterward. And there was something else on the tray, too, when we first saw it. Something not connected with food. But I can't remember—"

He screwed his face up, trying to picture how the tray had looked when they first saw it, but the images slid away too quickly to grasp.

"Here." Emma pushed a piece of paper at him. "Try and draw it. That's what I do when I can't remember something."

Tom scrawled a rectangle on the paper and then a circle inside it. "That's the dish. Bright red plastic, with a spoon to match. And there was a dishcloth here. It was folded up in the beginning." He sketched it in. "And over *here*—" His pen hovered over the paper, but he didn't know what to draw. "There was another bright thing—but not red. Yellow, maybe. And tall."

"I remember that." Robert nodded. "It was a drink. One of those plastic sports bottles with a top you can suck."

"Oh, yes." Tom was vaguely disappointed. He'd been certain it was something odder. He drew another, smaller, circle on his diagram and frowned down at the space that was left. "Oh, and there was a pair of scissors, too."

"*Scissors?*" Emma said. "What were they for?"

Tom shrugged. "No idea."

Robert reached over and took the pen out of his hand. "They were for cutting," he said in an odd voice. Carefully he drew in the scissors—and then another circle next to them. "Don't you remember, Tosh? There were three bright colors. Red and yellow and—"

"And blue," Tom said slowly. That was it. The thing he'd been trying to remember. "There was a ball of *blue wool* on the tray. Just like—"

"Just like the wool she used for that braid on the sports bag." Robert put the pen down, very carefully, on Emma's bedside table. He stared at the diagram. "Was it still there when you saw the tray again?"

Tom shook his head. "Only the scissors."

"Lorn's in that house somewhere," Robert said stubbornly. "We've got to go back and look again."

"But how can we?" said Tom. "They've already threatened you with the police. They've even got a picture of you."

"What do you want me to do?" Robert said fiercely.

"Walk away and forget all about it? Suppose there's something *really* bad going on in that house? If there *is* a room under the floor, maybe Lorn's a prisoner down there. A *hostage*."

"Oh come on, Robbo. You're getting carried away. It's not going to be anything like that," Tom said. And he laughed—but it was a nervous laugh. Robert was getting things out of proportion. Just because there was a hole under the floor, it didn't mean—

But Robert and Emma weren't laughing. They were both looking at him with sad, steady eyes. Almost pitying.

"How come you're so sure?" Emma said. "You think bad things never happen?"

"You think all the stuff you read in the papers is fiction?" said Robert.

Tom shuffled uncomfortably. "No, of course not. But it doesn't happen everywhere, does it? Not all the time. There's probably a very dull explanation for all this."

"Let's find out," Emma said briskly. "We're not going to discover anything by talking. We need to figure out how we're going to take a look inside that secret room."

"So how are you going to do that?" Tom said. "Knock on the front door and ask them to let you in?"

Emma raised her eyebrows at him. "What's the matter? Scared?"

Her voice was starting to get spiky. Hag-like. *She hasn't changed at all*, Tom thought. *She wants to tell both of us what to do.*

"Of course he's scared," Robert said impatiently. "You'd be scared, too, if you'd seen that man. But it doesn't mean we're giving up. We want to find out what's going on inside that house, just as much as you do. Don't we, Tosh?"

"If we can," Tom said cautiously.

"We need a double-pronged attack." Emma leaned forward and lowered her voice. "If we skip school tomorrow morning, and I borrow Helga . . ."

18

IT SOUNDED LIKE A BRILLIANTLY SIMPLE PLAN. *I'll go to the front door and distract them, and then you two can take a good look around the back. And if you can't find a way in—then maybe Helga will find one for me.* Even though it came from Emma, Tom was happy to give it a try. He was even prepared to cut school—because that meant Warren would be out. And one of his parents, too, with any luck.

The only problem was that Emma didn't have a clue about dogs. She thought Helga could be passed around like a parcel, and she expected her to trot along obediently, like a little wooden dog on wheels, doing exactly what she was told. The real Helga was a bit of a shock.

When Tom handed over her leash on Monday morning, Helga went crazy.

It wasn't Helga's fault. Tom had taken her for her usual early walk and then pretended to go off to school. When he came sneaking back—as soon as the house was empty— Helga thought she was in for a wonderful treat. Especially when she found they were going out again. She'd bounced through the front door, grinning ecstatically and licking any bit of Tom that she could reach.

And then he'd given her leash to Emma. Of all people.

She started barking reproachfully, straining at the leash and growling when Emma bent down to talk to her.

"What's gotten into her?" Robert said. "She's such a friendly dog. What's she got against Emma?"

Tom tried not to remember all the times he and Helga had shadowed Robert and Emma. The times he'd muttered and grumbled in Helga's ear. *Hag! Bite her ears off, Helga! Chase her into a bog! Rip up her tights!* Helga might not have understood the words, but she wasn't stupid. She knew exactly what Tom thought about Emma.

What he *used* to think.

"She's going to ruin the whole plan," Emma said crossly. "Do something, Tom."

There was only one thing Tom could think of. He edged cautiously up to Emma. "Sorry about this, but it's the quickest way." He gave her a huge grin and then put a tentative arm around her shoulders.

"You might as well do it properly," Emma said briskly. Without letting go of the leash, she turned around and gave him a quick, hard hug. "Do you think she's got the message now?"

Somehow Tom managed to catch his breath. "I hope so," he said. And then—in case Emma took that the wrong way—"Just don't snap. She won't like that. Be nice to me."

"That's going to be really tough," Emma said. She grinned. "Anything to keep the dog happy, though."

"She's not called The Dog. Her name's Helga." Tom bent down and gave Helga a pat. "Go with Emma now. All right? She's a friend."

Helga gave him a wary look, but she stopped pulling at the leash. She watched as Tom and Robert climbed onto their bikes and let them go without anything more than a whine.

"D'you think she'll be all right?" Robert looked back anxiously as they cycled away.

"She'll be fine," Tom said. "She's been on buses before."

"I didn't mean Helga. I meant Em."

That was a new one. Robert looking after Emma. Tom tried not to laugh.

"No need to worry about Emma," he said. "We're the ones taking risks. We'll be lucky if we get through this without being caught."

ONCE THEY'D HIDDEN THEIR BIKES ON THE WASTE GROUND, they were up on the embankment in a couple of minutes. Immediately, Robert began to thread his way through the brambles and the tangled hawthorn bushes. It took Tom a while to realize that they were following exactly the same track they'd used on Saturday night.

"How can you remember?" he hissed next time they stopped. "It all looks the same to me."

Robert grunted. "Practice. Now shut up, or someone's going to hear us."

He didn't stop again until they were level with the top of the cypress trees. Then he took out his phone to let Emma know they'd reached the back of the Armstrongs' house.

"Hang on a minute," Tom muttered. "Let's have a look first."

It was a shock to see the conservatory looking so—ordinary. He'd been thinking about it for thirty-six hours, almost without stopping, and it had grown and distorted in his mind, turning into an evil cartoon full of dark shadows and threatening corners. But it was just a conservatory. The windows were clean. The floor was polished. The furniture was neatly arranged, with the chair pushed in at the table and the television standing square in the middle of the red rug.

But the television was still running, with nobody watching it.

The French windows leading into the house were slightly open. He tried to peer past them, into the shadowy room beyond. He could just make out a couple of sofas and a table, but it was too dark to see any details.

Robert was watching him. "Ready?"

Tom nodded and began to work his way down the slope toward the fence at the bottom. It all seemed quite different in the daylight. He couldn't believe that they'd been brave—or stupid—enough to risk going over the fence and into the garden. He looked through a gap in the wood, but all he could see was the side of the rock garden.

Then Robert slid down, too, and they crouched side by side, waiting for the sound of the doorbell.

They heard Helga first, barking as she came down the road. Then the crunch of Emma's feet on the gravel path and the sound of the doorbell. It was impossible to see who answered the door. They just had to hope there was no one else in the house.

"Hello," Emma said, very high and loud, to make sure they heard it. "I'm sorry to bother you, but I'm doing a sponsored cycle ride—"

That was their signal. They hauled themselves up and over the fence at top speed, getting down into the cover of the cypresses as soon as they could. Robert stayed there, watching, but Tom ran forward and tried the door of the conservatory.

It was locked.

He wasn't exactly surprised, but he was disappointed. He and Robert had no chance of sneaking in while Emma was at the front door. They'd have to leave it all up to her. All he could do was give her a chance.

He took out the little, high-pitched whistle that he used to call Helga in the park. Bending as close as he could to the conservatory door, he blew long-short-long, just as he always did. He wasn't quite sure how Helga would react, but he knew she would make a fuss. She was a very excitable dog.

There was an eager yelp and then a shout from Emma.

"Maisie! Come back!"

Helga obviously didn't respond to that. She wasn't meant to. She was meant to race into the house, to give Emma an excuse to follow.

It was good in theory—but they hadn't realized that all the inside doors would be open. Helga made straight for the conservatory and the sound of the whistle. She appeared suddenly between the French windows, knocking them wider apart as she flew through, and Tom just had time to fling himself to the ground before Emma and the woman came racing in after her.

He cowered against the bricks, sure that the woman would spot him. Inside the conservatory, Helga was going crazy, jumping up at the windows and barking as loud as she could. Even above the noise of the television, Tom could hear the thuds as her body landed against the glass. Any moment now, the woman would look through the window to see what Helga was after.

But it didn't happen. The woman didn't seem to be interested in anything except getting rid of Helga. Tom could hear her flapping around and shouting ineffectually.

"Get out of here! Shoo! Go away!"

Emma was calling, too—from the other side of the conservatory. "Here, Maisie. Good dog. Come here."

None of that had any effect, of course. Helga just grew more and more frantic. Tom couldn't see what was happening, and he didn't dare lift his head to look. He just hoped nobody was going to hurt Helga.

Emma started giving instructions. "Try and keep her up by the window. Then I can sneak around and get her collar. No, don't look at me. You'll give it away. Just keep shouting."

Tom heard their voices through the wall, mixed with the noise of the television. He lay with his face against the bricks, feeling angry and frustrated. Emma hadn't had time to look at anything inside the house after all. And he and Robert had come all the way along the embankment for nothing.

Helga's barking changed, and Tom guessed that Emma had caught hold of her leash. There were yelps of protest as she was dragged away from the window. Then the French windows were closed firmly, and the sitting room door was slammed shut.

So that was it. Helga had bolted into the house and been recaptured—and they hadn't found out anything at all. What a waste of energy.

Tom turned around to crawl back to the hedge—and saw Robert at the conservatory door. *It's locked*, he mouthed. *You can't—* But Robert ignored him and pressed the handle down.

And the door opened in front of him.

19

"Shhh!" Lorn said frantically. "Be quiet!" She reached up quickly and put a hand over Bando's mouth. "It's a secret."

But Bando was nearly as frantic as she was. He grabbed her hand and pulled it away. "You *mustn't* go through there, Lorn! The monster will get you!"

"Shhh. It's all right," Lorn said. "I'm safe. Nothing happened."

"But it *might*." Bando wasn't going to be silenced. "You mustn't do it. You mustn't go in there again."

"OK, OK," Lorn said hastily. "We'll block up the hole. But only if you keep the secret. Is that a deal?"

Bando hesitated.

"Come on." Lorn shook his shoulder gently, wheedling now. "Don't you trust me?"

"Of course I do," Bando said.

"And you promise not to tell anyone?"

Bando hesitated again, and Lorn thought he was going to refuse, but he didn't. He gave a long sigh and said, "I promise."

"Good." Lorn tried not to sound relieved. "Let's block up the hole, then. Help me with the stone."

She took his hands and laid them underneath it, guiding him as he lifted it into place. When it was there, he stroked the front surface, feeling how the stone fitted into the wall. Lingering over the pointed lump that stuck out at the front.

"Feel that," he said "It's like a handle."

Lorn wanted to stop him from thinking about the stone. She turned away from it and changed the subject. "What are you doing down here, anyway? Were you looking for me?"

"Yes, I was. I—" For a moment Bando sounded vague. Then he remembered—and his voice came alive with excitement. "Yes! That's it! I saw you come down here. When I was by the woodpile. So I came to get you—but I then couldn't see where you were—"

"Never mind that," Lorn said quickly. "Just tell me what's going on."

Bando gave a delighted laugh. "They're here! Perdew's gone to fetch them into the cavern."

"Who's here?" Lorn had no idea what he was talking about.

"Cam!"

"What?"

"And—someone else, too." Bando was so gleeful that he could hardly get the words out. "They've come back!"

Lorn forgot how tired she was. *Robert*, said the voice in her head. *Oh, Robert.* She started across the storeroom—and then had to go back because Bando was shouting that he couldn't see the way. Catching his arm, she dragged him toward the ramp, peppering him with questions as they went.

"So what happened? How many of them have come back? Did they get where they were heading?"

"I don't know." That was the only answer Bando seemed to have. "I just heard Perdew say—and then he asked where you were. So I came to get you."

Lorn hauled him up the ramp. When they came out from behind the brazier, the others were all up at the far end of the cavern, crowded around the entrance. She raced toward them.

"Oh, *there* you are!" Dess said over his shoulder. "They couldn't get past the branches by themselves. So Perdew's gone to help them."

Lorn caught her breath. "They're very weak, then?"

"I think so." Dess pointed into the entrance tunnel. "Look."

Perdew's feet were just visible now. He was crawling backward out of the entrance tunnel, moving very slowly and carefully. Dragging someone after him, awkwardly, by the shoulders.

Shang and Ab went in closer, to help him and to take the weight. As they bent down, Lorn saw that it was Cam they were lifting. She was pale and unconscious, and her face was completely white, except for a long, raw wound that ran down one cheek and under her jaw. When Shang and Ab lifted her up, her arms fell loosely over theirs. Lorn was shocked to see how thin they were, and she stepped forward and touched one. It was cold under her hand.

"Bat furs!" she said quickly. "Get her down by the brazier and warm her up. She needs people under the covers, too. You, Annet. And Tina on the other side."

They moved fast. Half a dozen of them went down the cavern with Cam, and Bando and Dess moved into place to help with the next person. Lorn stayed where she was, watching Perdew dive back into the entrance tunnel.

Robert . . . she thought again.

But it wasn't Robert. It was Zak.

When they lifted him out of the tunnel, he looked old and dead. His face was waxy and his mouth hung open. Lorn shouted frantically at Perdew.

"Get him warm! Take Bando with you, and get him under the furs."

She turned back, peering eagerly into the entrance. But it was empty now. There was no one else coming into the cavern. Nate wasn't there; nor was Robert.

Only Cam and Zak had come back from the journey.

They laid the two of them side by side, near the brazier but not too near. Lorn made sure Zak had furs, too, and people to warm him with their body heat. Even though he didn't look as if he would ever move again.

Cam was almost as weak. Lorn crouched in front of her, gently rubbing Cam's cold hands. She tucked them into her own armpits and felt the chill seep through her body.

"Wake up, Cam," she said softly. "You're safe now. Wake up and tell us what happened."

Perdew was leaning over Zak, cupping his face in both hands. "Can you hear me? Open your eyes, Zak."

It was half an hour before either of them responded. But in that time, gradually, the color came back into their faces. Lorn could see their joints loosening and easing as their bodies grew warmer.

She was going to leave them to sleep, but Cam stirred suddenly and opened her eyes. Slowly her head turned, looking around the cavern. Then her jaw moved awkwardly. When she managed to speak at last, her voice was as rough as bitter-nut bark.

"Anything . . . to eat?"

Annet brought some hot mash, and Lorn lifted a little and put it to Cam's lips. Cam sucked the food off Lorn's fingers, but after a few mouthfuls, she turned her head away and fell asleep.

Lorn lowered her onto the bundled furs and then swiveled around to look at Zak. He was still unconscious, but Perdew had raised him up, to help him breathe. He was half lying and half sitting, propped between Shang and Bando.

Bando was frowning nervously. "That's what they look like when they're dead," he whispered.

"Nobody's going to die," Lorn said firmly. Willing it to be true. "They'll be all right when we've gotten them warm and given them some food."

She put a hand on Zak's forehead. It was colder than she had expected, clammy and damp.

"Wake up," she said. "You're home now, Zak. You're safe."

His mouth tightened, infinitesimally. Slowly his eyelids lifted, and Lorn found herself staring straight into his eyes. They were blue and very clear, and she could see her own face reflected in the pupils, small and distant, like a face looking up from the bottom of a pit. His eyes sharpened, focusing on her face. Looking at her.

And it felt . . . it felt like . . .

A hand on her head, moving gently.
Not making patterns, just smoothing her hair while she
stayed still and still and still, keeping the feeling.
To remember afterward, down in the dark.

"Zak?" she said uncertainly. "What's happening? Do you know——?"

But his eyes closed again before he could answer her.

2 O

TOM AND ROBERT KNEW EXACTLY WHAT TO DO. EMMA HAD made them practice it over and over again, all Sunday afternoon, until it was fast and slick. They could manage the whole thing in ten seconds now.

The television first. They lifted it up, with its table, moving it smoothly to the left. The instant they put it down, Tom fell on his knees and started rolling up the red rug. His fingers felt fat and clumsy, and there was a depressing, discouraging voice whining away in his head (*There's not enough time—she's going to come back and catch us—how can Emma keep her away?*), but it didn't slow him down. After all their rehearsing, the actions were automatic.

As soon as the rug was rolled back enough, Robert started undoing the rotating catches that held the lid in place. There were four of them, sunk into the wood, one on each side. He swung them open and slid his fingertips under one edge of the lid. Tom finished rolling the rug and leaned forward to help him. Together, they lifted the heavy lid out of the way.

And the black space opened up in front of them.

It was much bigger than Tom had expected. Bigger and deeper and darker. The air inside was stale and squalid, smelling of earth and mold and cheap air freshener. Robert took a flashlight out of his pocket and shone it down at the bottom of the hole. It was covered with black plastic, ripped in a couple of places, and it was too far down to reach from where they were.

"Look quickly!" Tom muttered. "We've got to get out of here." He knew it was stupid to speak, but he couldn't stop himself. This was the dangerous, unpredictable part of the operation.

Robert made a face at him and then leaned farther into the hole, angling the flashlight left. There was a quick rustle from that direction. And then silence.

Rats, Tom thought. He went down flat on the ground, sticking his head into the opening and looking along the shiny plastic. Beyond the pool of light from Robert's flashlight, he could see more space, going back all the way to the house. He reached up and took the light so that he could shine it to the far end.

And he saw—something.

Someone.

There was a crouching figure huddled into the far corner, close against the foundation of the house. Its head was turned away, and it had both hands pressed tightly over its mouth. But, above the hands, he could see the glint of its eyes looking sideways at him.

"Hello?" he said softly. Stupidly. He could hear his voice shaking.

The head shifted slightly, turning farther away. The eyes couldn't see him now, but the creature's whole body was tense. Until that moment, Tom hadn't been able to tell anything except that it was human. Now he could see that it—

she—was a small, thin girl, maybe seven or eight years old, with pale skin and peculiar, matted hair.

She was wearing a strange collection of garments layered one over another, but her legs were bare, and her feet and hands were much darker than the rest of her skin. She looked terrified.

Robert nudged him out of the way, edging in so that he could see as well. But as he put his head through the opening, Emma's voice came through from the hall, very loud and clear.

"I'm really sorry to have been such a nuisance. I do apologize for my dog."

That was a signal. It meant that she couldn't spin it out any longer. She was standing in the doorway, with her foot on the threshold—and they had to get out of the conservatory as fast as they could.

There was no time to think. Nothing else they could do. Tom grabbed Robert's shoulder and pulled, expecting him to resist. But he didn't. He was on his feet instantly, reaching for the lid. The two of them dropped it back into place and Robert knelt down to fasten the catches. In less than ten seconds, everything was just as it had been before they came, with the rug spread neatly over the opening and the television standing on top of it.

The moment it was done, Tom darted through the door and ran for the hedge. He assumed that Robert would be right behind him, but when he looked around, he saw him still at the conservatory door, fumbling at the lock. Leaning out of the hedge, Tom beckoned frantically.

Robert turned around and flew, crossing the narrow strip

of grass at top speed and throwing himself into the hedge. He didn't stop to say anything to Tom. He went up the nearest tree and over the fence in almost a single movement.

Tom looked back nervously. As he did so, Emma's voice floated over from the front of the house.

"Good-bye, then. Thanks for the chat."

Helga barked, the front door banged shut—and Tom hauled himself up the tree and over the fence, as fast as he could. He came down on Robert's back and rolled clear, landing in an ungainly sprawl.

Robert was on all fours, with his head bent, shaking and retching. His face was white, and he'd just been sick in a patch of brambles. Tom sat up and looked at him.

"Is it her?" he said.

Robert nodded and sat back, wiping his mouth. "But she's—" He shook his head and stopped, turning his face away.

Tom didn't know what to say. He was trembling, too, and his head was full of desperate, urgent questions. But it wasn't the right time to ask them. He crawled back to the fence and put his eye to a crack in the wood, looking back at the house.

The woman was just walking through the French windows, into the conservatory. Tom tensed, trying to see if there was anything wrong, anything to show that he and Robert had been there. But the woman didn't even glance around. She went down on her hands and knees beside the television, with her head close to the floor. He was too far away to hear what she was saying, but he could see her lips moving and her head bobbing about. After a couple of minutes, she stood up and brushed off her skirt. Then she went out through the sitting room, pulling the French windows almost shut behind her.

Tom turned around, to describe what he'd seen—but Robert had gone. He was already moving up the embankment, squirming forward on his stomach. For a second, Tom wanted to yell after him. *We can't just go! What are we going to do?* But Robert didn't look back. He wriggled behind a clump of bushes, and Tom had to scramble to catch up before he lost sight of him.

Robert didn't stop until he was back on the piece of waste ground beyond the houses, pulling his bike out of the bushes.

"What are we going to do?" Tom said, panting up behind him.

"Not yet," Robert said grimly. He was already on his bike. "Let's get home first."

He didn't speak again until they reached his house. And then it was only, "Around the back!" as he headed for the side gate. Tom went patiently after him, propping his bike against the side wall of the house and following him into the kitchen.

Helga came bombing through from the front of the house and flung herself at his ankles, barking hysterically. He went down on his knees and let her lick his face all over. It was a relief to have something familiar and safe and normal.

"Yes, yes," he said. "Good dog. You're a heroine."

"*I'm* a heroine," Emma said from the doorway. "Have you got any idea how hard it was to go on talking to that woman?"

"Did you find out anything new?" Robert said. He was

quite different now. Cool and controlled. Totally focused on Emma's answer.

She shrugged. "All pretty negative. No, she doesn't like dogs. No, they don't do barbecues. No, she hasn't got a daughter—she was very sharp about that one. Told me right off the bat, the moment I mentioned the word. How about you? Did you manage to open up that place under the floor?"

"There's a girl down there," Robert said baldly. "Shut in, so she can't get out."

Emma stared at him for a moment without speaking. Then she pulled out a chair and sat down, very slowly. "Is it Lorn?"

"I think so." Robert nodded. "She's certainly *like* Lorn. And her hair's full of weird braids."

"I didn't really think—" Emma took a long breath. "Are you *sure* she's shut in? She wasn't just playing some kind of game?"

"No," Robert said shortly. He looked across at Tom. "Tell her, Tosh."

Tom stood up, keeping hold of Helga's collar. He wanted to explain to Emma what the hole in the ground was like. He wanted to make her smell the air and imagine the way the girl had crouched against the far wall, looking strange and terrified. He wanted her to feel the shock of it. But he didn't know how to communicate that.

So he just said, "Robbo's right. They're keeping her a prisoner."

Emma shook her head slowly, as though she couldn't believe it. "Who is she? How did she get there?"

Tom shrugged. "How should we know? But we'll find out, won't we? When the police get her out."

"No!" Robert was almost shouting. "We're not going to tell the police."

Tom couldn't believe it. "We can't just leave her there."

"We've got to get her out." That was Emma.

"Of course we're going to get her out," Robert said impatiently. "But we don't want the police involved. They'll whisk her off and put her in foster care or in a hospital or something like that."

"Isn't that where she ought to be?" said Tom, remembering the girl's pale face and stick-thin arms and legs. "She needs people to look after her."

"*We'll* look after her," Robert said. "We'll get her out of there and take her to the woods. Nothing will do her any good until she's back together."

"How are you going to do that?" Emma said. "The trick with Helga won't get you into the house again."

"We don't need that." Robert put a hand into his pocket. "We can get in whenever we like." He held out his hand, balled up like a fist, and opened the fingers slowly, one by one.

Lying in his palm was the key to the Armstrongs' conservatory.

21

"WE CAN'T DO IT," EMMA SAID. "WE CAN'T JUST TAKE things into our own hands."

"You don't understand!" Robert said fiercely. "Nor do you, Tosh. You've always had someone around to bail you out: Mom and Dad, doctors, experts—people like that. You don't know what it's like to face real danger. When there's no one except you to take responsibility."

"There *are* people," Tom said. "All we've got to do is make a phone call."

"That might save the girl under the floor. But it won't help Lorn." Robert was leaning forward urgently now, with his elbows on the table. "And Lorn's the one who needs help first. Because if we don't rescue her—she'll die."

Lorn's not real, Tom wanted to say. *Not the way that other girl is real.*

But he didn't feel so certain anymore. The pale girl in the black room seemed just as remote and fantastic as the little people living under the ground. If one thing was true, why not the other?

"Look," Robert said desperately, "give me twenty-four hours. That's all I need. After that you can go to the police— if you still want to." He watched Tom's and Emma's faces, turning the conservatory key over and over in his long, strong fingers. "Just help me get that girl out of there first, so I can take her to the woods. We could do it tonight."

"You think so?" Emma said impatiently. "Just because you've got that key? That's not the answer to everything. What about the security light? And burglar alarms? I bet they've got one of those."

"There must be a way to deal with things like that." Robert's face was stubborn. "We've just got to think."

But Emma hadn't finished. "And suppose you succeed and Lorn—*comes back together*. What happens then? Does she have to go home to that hole in the ground?"

"Of course not. I'll look after her."

"Oh yes?" Emma raised her eyebrows. "So will you be wanting Mom and Dad to adopt her?"

"How should I know?" Robert was starting to look annoyed now. "We can't worry about details like that—"

"Yes, we can, Rob." Emma shook her head at him. "You've got to *think*."

Tom wanted to shake her and make her be quiet. *Same old hag*, he thought. *Still trying to take charge*. But then he saw her expression—and a switch flipped in his head. She wasn't putting Robert down because she liked to. She was trying to take charge because she was afraid.

He could understand that. He was afraid, too.

"Look, Robbo," he said. "We've got to be practical. Emma's right about the burglar alarm. They're bound to have one of those. And they're bound to be on their guard when they find that the key's disappeared."

"They'll think *I* stole it," Emma said grimly.

At last something seemed to register with Robert. He sat back on his heels, looking thoughtful. "If they're really worried, they might get the lock changed. I need to get the key copied, don't I? And try and sneak the original one back before anyone notices."

Emma gave a short, harsh bark of laughter. "So who are you now? The Invisible Man? Stop daydreaming, Rob. None of it's going to work. Not unless you've got a double agent on the inside?"

Robert had no answer for that. But it sparked off something in Tom's mind.

"Not a double agent," he said slowly. "But there's someone on the inside who might be . . . persuaded to help us. If we have a little talk with him."

IT WAS EASY TO HANG AROUND BY THE BUS STOP WHEN THE school buses came through. Robert went ahead, to stand at the corner of the street, and Tom and Emma watched the buses come past.

Warren was on the third one. He got off with a crowd of other boys, but Tom could see he was really on his own, just tagging along at the back. The others went up the road in little groups, chatting and fooling around, and Warren trailed along behind them, laughing self-consciously whenever he overheard a joke.

"The others aren't a problem," Tom muttered to Emma. "They'll shake him off in a minute, when they start going different ways. We just need to wait for the right moment."

They strolled along behind Warren, watching the other boys pull away from him. Gradually a gap opened up. By the time Warren reached his street, he was three or four steps behind the others.

Robert was standing on the corner, pretending to make a phone call. He let the others go past and then stepped out, immediately in front of Warren, so close that their noses were almost touching—or they would have been if Robert hadn't been a good six inches taller.

It was meant to be threatening, and it was. And Warren reacted just as Tom thought he would. He stopped dead for a moment, looking down at the pavement. Then he took a step backward and tried to walk around Robert, with his face turned away.

It was the instinctive defense of someone who expected to be a victim. And it didn't work. Robert simply stepped sideways to block his path, and Tom came up behind and tapped him on the shoulder.

"Hi, Warren," he said. "Fancy seeing you here."

Warren stopped dead. Then he turned around, slowly and warily, and looked at Tom's face. As the message traveled from his eyes to his brain, his hand went up to his bag and the fingers clamped tightly around the strap.

"That's right," Tom said cheerfully. "I'm the one who stole your bag. But it was very disappointing. I was hoping for something much better inside."

Warren's eyes flicked nervously left and right. *Not too fast*, Tom told himself. *If he gets really scared, he'll bolt.* They had to do things quietly, without attracting attention. He took the key out of his pocket, producing it with a flourish, to make sure that Warren was really looking.

"Recognize this?" he said, waggling it in the air.

Warren looked blank. *Oh come on, you lunkhead. You must*

know what it is. But Tom spelled it out, to make sure it was crystal clear.

"It's a key to your house, Warren. And do you know what it unlocks?" He waggled it again. "It's the key of the conservatory."

Warren's eyes widened suddenly. His hand flashed out, and he grabbed at the key, trying to twist it out of Tom's hand. But he wasn't quick enough. Tom threw it over his head, and Robert snatched it out of the air and put it in his pocket.

"Don't be mean," Emma cooed. She stepped into the gutter, moving up beside Warren so that he was completely boxed in. "Let him have it back." She gave Warren a big, artificial smile. "You don't want us poking around in the conservatory, do you?"

Warren's mouth began to tremble, and Tom wondered for a second what would happen if they just told him the truth. *We know about the girl under the floor. We're going to rescue her. Will you help us?*

That would be the clean, direct way. But they couldn't take the risk.

He looked kindly at Warren and gave him a smile like Emma's. "Of course you can have the key back," he crooned. "We're not interested in that cruddy old television in your conservatory. I'm sure you've got much better things *inside* the house. Haven't you?"

Warren shook his head furiously. And then nodded, as if he didn't know what answer to give.

Tom raised his voice slightly, giving it a threatening edge.

"I hope you're going to help us. Otherwise . . . we might have to talk to your sister." Warren's face went white. For a second, Tom thought he'd overdone it and ruined the whole thing.

Then Warren said, "I haven't got a sister." His voice sounded tight, as if someone was choking him.

"There's a girl around somewhere," Emma said gaily. She reached out toward his bag and flicked at the braid on the zipper toggle. "If you won't help us, we'll have to track her down and see if she's more cooperative."

Warren stayed dumb, looking down at his feet.

"Well?" Tom said. "Are you going to help us?"

He knew the answer already. It was obvious from the way Warren was standing and from his sullen, hopeless expression. They'd gotten him exactly where they wanted him, and all he needed now was a bit more hassling to make him admit it.

"What do you want?" Warren muttered without looking up.

"That's better," Tom said. "That's *much* better. Now you're being sensible—and we can talk about the key."

He clicked his fingers and Robert tossed it to him. He caught it and held it high in the air, dangling it just out of Warren's reach.

"I'm going to give this to you," he said. "And I want you to put it back in the door, very quietly. So that no one knows it's been missing. Can you do that?"

Warren gave a reluctant, sulky nod and held out his hand for the key.

"Not so fast." Tom lifted it higher. "There's another thing as well. We'd like a little bit of help tonight."

Warren's eyes flickered up and down, left and right. He looked everywhere except into Tom's face. "I can't do anything," he whispered. "My dad would kill me."

"Then we'll have to look for your sister after all," Emma said sweetly.

Warren's face went bright red. "What have I got to do?" he said.

"We want you to turn off the burglar alarm," said Tom. "And the security light. Just for tonight. We'd like them off by midnight."

"No, no, not midnight. I can't—" Warren shook his head. "They're not always asleep—"

"Two o'clock, then?" Tom looked at him sternly.

Warren nodded. Tom had the feeling that he would have agreed to anything.

"Don't forget," Robert said from behind him. "And don't even think about telling anyone." It was the first time he'd spoken. Warren glanced fearfully over his shoulder, and Robert drew a finger slowly across his throat.

"Look at me!" Tom said sharply. Warren's head snapped back. Tom pushed the key into his hand and closed the fingers around it. "Here you are, then. Put it back as soon as you get home—without being noticed. And make sure you don't fall asleep tonight. If the burglar alarm goes off"—he smiled wolfishly—"we'll have to call the police and tell them about all the suspicious things we've seen."

He meant to sound vague and terrifying, and he could see

that he'd succeeded. He stared straight into Warren's eyes, not letting him look away, and Warren stared back, beyond thinking or speaking or moving. Paralyzed with fear.

For one, long moment, Tom knew exactly what it felt like. He could have been staring right through Warren's pudgy face into his wretched, shivering mind. It was like being in a tight, closed space, with no air and no room to move.

"All right," he said abruptly. Ending it sooner than he meant to because he couldn't bear the feeling anymore. "You can go now. Just do what you're told and keep quiet about it. Then you won't get into trouble."

Warren bobbed his head obediently, and looked around for a way out. Emma gave him another one of her smiles.

"I know we can rely on you, Warren," she said. Then she stepped back and let him dodge past her, into his street.

They heard him scuttle down toward his house, getting slower as he reached the end of the road.

"He'll never do it," Robert said.

"Yes, he will." Emma grinned at Tom. "You played that just right. He'd have done anything he was told. You had him in the palm of your hand."

Tom felt sick. He'd *made* Warren do what he wanted. Instinctively, he'd known the right things to say and the right tone of voice to use, to tap into the fear that dominated everything Warren did. He'd *understood* him.

It was like a lead weight in his mind.

2 2

"NATE'S . . . *dead?*" LORN SAID SLOWLY.

She said it for them all because no one else could speak the word out loud. The cavern was silent with the shock of it.

Cam nodded and closed her eyes for a moment, exhausted by the effort of telling them. For almost half an hour she had been talking about the journey, ignoring questions and explaining everything that had happened, in order. She was very pale, except for the jagged red wound running down her face.

And she'd told less than half of it. They still didn't know what had happened to Robert.

Bando wriggled closer to Lorn, and Annet began to cry quietly, with her face in her hands. Twisting her fingers together, Lorn tried not to picture how Nate had died. Tried not to think about the hot, stinking breath of the hedge-tiger and how its black eyes must have sharpened suddenly as its yellow teeth snapped together.

It was Perdew who broke the silence. "Is Robert dead, too?" he said harshly.

Cam rolled her head sideways, looking to Zak for an answer. He let his eyes travel around the cavern, from the big stack of new wood to the padded blankets Lorn had made out of white floss. He gazed at the fresh green leaves they were eating and the little sacs of juice piled into snail shells beside Annet. When he spoke, his voice was hoarse and dry.

"You didn't collect all that food yourselves, did you?"

For a moment it sounded as though he was talking about something completely different. People glanced uneasily at each other, and Perdew shifted impatiently, wanting his question answered.

And then—Lorn understood. The thought came so suddenly that she realized it had been there all the time, at the back of her mind. She'd been pushing it away.

"It's Robert, isn't it?" she said. "He's the one who brings the food."

Zak didn't answer. Nor did Cam. But the others stared at her.

"How *can* it be Robert?" Ab said. "It's impossible."

"No, it's not." Lorn struggled to keep her voice steady. "Don't you remember why they all went on that terrible journey? Robert was trying to get back to—what he was before. And he's done it. *He's stopped being small.*"

There was a breathless, disbelieving silence. Then Cam nodded slowly—and the cavern exploded. People pushed forward, talking and laughing and shouting, breaking the circle to get as close as they could to Zak and Cam.

"Is it true? Is it really true?"

"How did he do it?"

"Why was it only Robert?"

"What about us?"

"What do we have to do—?"

Lorn found herself on her own, outside the crowd, looking at people's backs. *Why are you all so desperate to be big?* she wanted to yell. *Why can't you stay like this?*

Their heads were full of pictures from *before*, from the lost time that was too dangerous to think about unless Zak made them do it. But inside her own head, there was nothing. Only darkness.

We don't remember, she wanted to shout. *We look forward.* But she knew that no one would listen to that now. For the first time since Zak brought her into the cavern, she felt as if she didn't belong. As if she would never belong again. Robert had left and gone where she couldn't reach him, and now all the others wanted to leave, too.

And she couldn't want that. She didn't know how.

She slid backward out of the broken circle, desperate to get away from the voices and the questions and the terrible *desire*. Grabbing a bundle of bat furs, she made for the entrance tunnel, not following any plan, but acting instinctively. Taking the nearest escape route.

As soon as she pulled out the branches, she began to feel the cold. By the time she was halfway through, her skin felt as though it was shrinking around her. She was shivering uncontrollably, and her teeth knocked together, every breath drawing icy air into the very center of her body. When she came out into the woods, she was already chilled, right through to her bones.

Outside, it was even colder. The earth was covered with sharp white crystals that hurt her feet as she clambered over them. *I can't*, she thought. *I can't—* And she nearly turned back.

Then a breath of wood smoke came drifting down toward her, and she realized where she could find some heat. Following the scent of the smoke, she turned and clambered up toward the little hole where it escaped from the cavern.

Even there, the ground was very cold, but it was warmer than anywhere else. Spreading a couple of furs underneath her, she wrapped the others around her body, drawing a fold across her face to keep in the warm breath. Only her eyes were left uncovered. She stared out at the cold from inside a cocoon of fur.

The woods were beautiful and strange. The cold white crystals edged each separate clod of earth and every bare twig. They outlined the stray, brittle leaves still hanging on the great trees and coated the dead stems of the small ones.

If she lifted her chin out of the fur, she could see her own breath eddying out into the air, like the smoke from the brazier. For the first time, she wondered where it came from, thinking how it went in cold and came out warm. She imagined a labyrinth of dark tunnels inside her body where the change happened slowly, magically. Time after time.

Drawing another breath of the icy air, she lowered her head to blow it out over her cold fingers. And as she did that, something came drifting up from the bottom of her mind. Something fainter than the smell of wood smoke, harder to grasp than the breath itself. A voice that spoke right from the center of who she was.

Warm breath in the cold black room, blowing onto stiff fingers . . . The warmth is a thing you can trust,

like sweetness in the mouth and strings that wind
together. . . .
Like the colors that move in the air and the sounds that
come from up above . . .
. . . life, Jim, but not as we know it . . .
. . . where everybody knows your name . . .
The sounds come down, and the lips and tongue move in
the dark, trying to make those patterns . . .
But without any noise . . . shhh, hands over the mouth . . .
No noise, only the patterns . . .

"Lorn?" Zak said, from somewhere far away. "Lorn, you'll die if you stay there."

She opened her eyes and came swimming up out of the dark place where she had been. Zak was standing over her, propping himself on a stick. His face was yellow and tired, and he was leaning heavily, swaying slightly as he looked down at her.

"You shouldn't be out here!" The shock of seeing him sent Lorn shooting back into the ordinary world. "You're not strong enough. You should be in the cavern."

"Come with me then." Zak held out his free hand.

She jumped up and took it quickly because she was afraid that he would fall. But he was looking hard at her, and his blue eyes were sharp and clear. She knew he wouldn't be distracted into thinking about himself.

"I can't go back," she said. "I can't bear it."

"Can't bear what?" he said. But she could tell that he knew. That he was pushing at her to say what she meant.

And because it was Zak, she told him. "I can't bear the way they're all remembering. Wanting to go back. How can I share that? There's nothing in my head except *here*. If I'm not in the cavern—then I'm nothing."

"*No* memories?" Zak said. "Are you *sure*?"

"Nothing I can understand. Nothing that makes sense. Only—"

She stopped because she wanted him to finish the sentence for her. She wanted him to tell her about the voice in her head, to say that it was nothing to worry over.

But all he said was, "Pick up the blankets."

The moment she had them, he began to move down the slope, very slowly, leaning on her arm so that she had to go with him. Step by step they made their way back to the cavern entrance, but as they knelt down to go in, Lorn caught the noise from inside. The others were still talking all at once, laughing with excitement. Letting go of Zak's arm, Lorn tried to draw back, but he caught hold of her hand and wouldn't let her go.

"If things don't make sense, that means you need to find out more," he said. "If you run away, you'll never figure it out."

Lorn bent her head, mumbling at the ground. "Suppose I'm better off not knowing?"

"I've never thought of you as a coward," Zak said.

His voice was so weak now, that she could hardly hear it. Getting him back into the cavern was more urgent than anything. She waved her hand at the entrance tunnel. "You go first. Then I can give you a push if you need it."

He gave her a wry, sideways smile, but he didn't argue.

Going down onto his belly, he slid into the tunnel, pulling himself forward with his arms. He managed without any help, but when he stood up inside the cavern, he was staggering with exhaustion. Lorn slid out after him and jumped up, putting a hand under his elbow.

"You shouldn't have come out," she said.

"If I hadn't come, you would have died."

She knew he was right. She would have slipped into a frozen sleep, with that strange, familiar voice going on and on in her head. *One of the patterns you can trust . . . Like sweetness in the mouth and strings that wind together . . .* It wouldn't have taken long to die out there in the cold. Zak had saved her life.

But it had taken all his energy. He was leaning heavily on her arm now, looking toward the corner by the brazier.

"Come on," Lorn said. "We've got to get warm." She started to lead him down the cavern.

"There you are." Perdew looked around as they went past. "So you weren't in the storeroom after all?"

"What?" Lorn stopped and stared at him. "What are you talking about?"

"Oh, it was Bando." Perdew grinned. "You know what he's like. He noticed you weren't in the cavern, and he got it in his head that you had to be down in the storeroom. For some reason he went charging down there to get you back."

"So where is he now?" Lorn said sharply.

Perdew shrugged. "Still down there, probably. Blundering around and knocking over all the grain heaps. Do you want me to go and find him?"

"No. No, I'll have to go." Lorn looked quickly at Zak. "I'm sorry—"

Zak just nodded and slipped his arm out of hers. "Off you go," he said gently.

She was off immediately, not waiting to explain to anyone. They could ask questions when she came back. What she had to do now was find Bando, as fast as she could.

Let him be in the storeroom. Please let him still be there.

She had no idea how long he'd been down there. But she knew exactly why he'd gone. The moment he thought she was in danger, he would have been off to rescue her.

Don't let him be in the tunnel. Let him still be blundering around.

He couldn't have found the opening. He *couldn't*. Not in the dark, with no one to show him the way. He would have had to feel his way all along the wall to find the right stone. Surely he wouldn't have done that?

But when she ran down into the storeroom, she knew at once that she was wrong. There was no one else in there. And even from the bottom of the ramp, she could feel the cold air seeping in.

The stone had been moved and the secret passage was open.

23

THEY'D ARRANGED TO LEAVE ROBERT'S HOUSE TOGETHER, at half past one. Tom lay on his bed, fully dressed under his duvet, and waited for the right time to sneak out and meet the other two.

He had no trouble staying awake. He felt as though he would never sleep again. Not now that he knew about the girl under the floor. They must all be in it together—Mr. and Mrs. Armstrong and Warren, too. What were they doing? Why did they keep her there?

His brain made lurid pictures of Mr. Armstrong, blown up to the size of a giant, with the girl standing in the palm of his hand. She stood and stretched, ready to run away, and his fingers closed around her, one by one. Not crushing her, but coming together like bars, to keep her where she was. Tom saw her tiny, pale face peering through the gaps between the fingers—until Mr. Armstrong's other hand moved across in front of it, stroking his curled fist.

You're mine. I'm keeping you safe. I won't let anything hurt you.

It was a terrible picture. Tom couldn't wait to wrestle those fingers open and snatch the girl away. She had to be rescued. If they couldn't get her out themselves, tonight, then they had to call the police. That was clear.

But were their plans good enough? Would they be able to do it?

It felt impossible, and horribly dangerous.

By quarter past one, his parents were asleep. It was easy to slide out of bed and down the stairs. The only tricky part was getting his bike out of the shed without making a noise. He did it slowly, being supercautious, and that made him late. It was just after half past one when he reached Robert's house.

Robert and Emma were already out on the pavement, a little way down the road. They both had their bikes, and Emma was wearing a bulging backpack. Tom knew what was inside that. They'd made very careful, detailed plans.

The three of them set off across the city, cycling one behind the other, without speaking. The streets in the center were eerily empty, with all the shops shuttered and the office blocks dark and silent.

Even when they reached the development, there was no one on the streets. There were lights in some of the houses, but it was too cold for loitering outside. Tom's fingers were almost numb, and when he touched the bare metal of his handlebars, it stung like fire.

They stopped just before they reached the Armstrongs' street. Robert unzipped Emma's backpack and took out an oilcan. Then he went ahead on his own, leaving Tom and Emma with the bikes.

"He ought to have gone along the embankment," Emma muttered under her breath. "It's too risky going through all those gardens. There might be dogs. And he's so clumsy."

Tom thought of Robert creeping along the street. Diving down the side of the nearest house and moving silently from garden to garden. "He'll be fine," he said reassuringly. "You haven't seen how good he is now. And he's only got to cross a few fences."

"How long will *that* take?"

Emma was trying to sound brittle and detached. A week ago, Tom would have thought, *Leave him alone, you hag*. But it was different now. He took a random guess, to comfort her.

"He should do it in ten minutes. Easily."

Emma looked at her watch and nodded briskly. "All right. We'll take a look in ten minutes. Now we'd better be quiet—unless someone comes along. We'll talk then, so we don't look suspicious."

Yes, ma'am, Tom thought. But he didn't say it.

It seemed a long ten minutes, with nothing to do and no talking. Emma looked at her watch a dozen times. After nine and a half minutes, she pushed the bikes at Tom and went to the corner. She came back very quickly, and when she spoke, her voice was shaking.

"The side gate's ajar. You'd better go."

Until that moment, Tom hadn't thought about leaving her alone in the dark. Suddenly he imagined what it would be like for her, waiting on and on, with nothing to do but look at her watch. "Do you want to go instead of me?" he whispered.

"No!" It was almost too loud for safety. "We have to stick to the plan. Get going."

"Well—shout if there's anything wrong." Tom wanted to tell her not to be frightened, but he didn't dare. He just passed the bikes over to her and went quickly and quietly around the corner and into the Armstrongs' street.

It was after two o'clock now, and all the houses were dark. He hurried down the road, trusting that no one was looking out at him. When he reached the far end, he stepped off the pavement and onto the grass in front of the Armstrongs' house.

Five slow, careful steps took him up to the side gate. He pushed cautiously at it, hoping that Robert had remembered to oil the hinges as well as the bolts. It opened as silently as a gate in a dream, and he stepped through it into the darkness of the back garden.

All the conservatory blinds were pulled shut, but around the edges he could see a glimmer of cold light from the television. The sound was turned down, but he could hear it faintly from outside. There was no sign of Robert, though— and nothing to show whether Warren had turned off the burglar alarm.

Tom's heart was beating so fast that he could hardly breathe. For a second, he was sure that the whole thing was a delusion. How could there be a room under the floor? How could there be a girl hidden down there? It was impossible.

Then he realized that he could hear the television only because the conservatory door was slightly open.

He crept up and put his eye to the opening. In the light from the television, he saw Robert on his knees on the red rug, with the side of his head against the floor. It took Robert a second to realize that Tom was there. When he did, he beckoned vigorously, pointing to his ear and then down at the ground.

Tom knelt down and listened. For a moment the noise of the television distracted him. He put a hand over one ear, to shut it out, and put the other ear against the floor. Through the wood, he heard a faint, high humming. Not a tune, but a long, wordless note that moved unsteadily around the same pitch.

It was true. There really was a girl down there.

Robert put a hand on Tom's arm, pulling him up. He tapped at his watch and then pointed to the television. Tom knew he was right. They had no idea what to expect when they tried to get the girl to move, but it made sense to open up the black room as quickly as possible.

They lifted the television out of the way and then Tom began to roll up the rug, glad of the rehearsed, familiar actions. But this time being quiet was more important than being fast. Robert took his time turning the catches on the lid, and when they were open, he raised the lid very slowly, letting the dim light filter down into the dark space underneath.

There was no humming now. The girl was completely silent.

Robert leaned over, putting his head right down into the hole. Tom heard a short, stifled sound, like someone breathing in quickly.

"Can you see her?" he whispered.

"I think she's up at the far end," Robert muttered. He sat back and swung his legs into the hole. "I don't want to use the flashlight if I can help it. I think it's better if I go in and get her."

"Don't frighten her," Tom whispered. Knowing it was a stupid thing to say. They had no idea how she was going to react to anything.

Robert let himself down into the hole. It was not big enough for him to stand upright. He had to bend over and shuffle forward.

"It's all right," he said softly. "We're your friends. We've come to rescue you."

There was a quick shuffling sound. And then another noise.

"Shhh."

Robert straightened up, with his head sticking through the hatch. "She just keeps moving backward. I don't want to make her yell. And I can't get her to look at me."

"Let me try." Tom stood back to let Robert out and then slid over the edge, into the hole.

It was very dark down there. And cold. And damp. The girl's face was a pale glimmer, in the far corner, where he'd seen her before. She was holding her head in the same way, sideways on to him, with her hands over her mouth.

There was a flashlight in his pocket, and he was tempted to switch it on, but it seemed like too much of a shock. He squatted down, to make himself look smaller and less intimidating, and hunted for something simple and soothing to say. The most obvious sound was the one she had already made herself.

"Shhh," he said. "Shhh."

The girl tilted her head slightly, moving her face away

from him. But her body leaned closer. He realized that she was turning her ear to catch the sound he made.

He said it again. "Shhh."

He was rewarded by a turn of her whole body. She twisted around, coming forward on her hands and knees, and presented him with the other ear.

"Shhh," he said. Was that the only word she understood?

Robert reached through the trapdoor, prodding at his back. "We've got to do something," he hissed. "We have to get her *out*."

The girl's head turned again, and she picked up the last word. "*Out*," she said. Her voice was very soft, and she spoke in a strange way, moving her tongue around in her mouth so that the word was blurred and strange.

Tom nodded and said it back to her. "Out. Yes?"

She began shuffling toward him, still on all fours, shaking off blankets and pushing them behind her. As she came closer, he was aware of a strong, sweet scent, like powder or cheap soap, with something stronger and sourer underneath it. She moved in very close, the way a small child would, putting her face up to Tom's and moving it around. For a second he thought she must have trouble with her eyes. Then he realized that she was sniffing at him.

"Shhhh," he murmured again. And then, "Out."

He began to back away, toward the trapdoor, holding his hands out for her to follow him. She edged forward suspiciously, stopping after each step, and Tom slowed down to keep pace with her, holding his breath as they reached the opening.

She put her head back and looked up, and he heard her

sniff again. And then stop, as she caught Robert's scent. She was breathing very fast now, and Tom could feel how tense she was.

He moved beyond the opening and gestured up at it, to show that she was free to go up on her own. But she clearly didn't understand what he meant. She looked across at him and then copied his gesture, watching her own hand. Frowning as she tried to puzzle it out.

"I think we're going to have to lift her up," Tom said softly. "Can you manage that, Robbo?"

Robert's head appeared in the space, blocking out most of the light. The girl tensed and shrank away, and Tom thought she was going to scuttle back to her corner.

"Shhh," he said soothingly.

"Come on," Robert said. He reached his long arms down into the space. "We only want you to come out."

The girl put a hand over her mouth again. "Out," she said between her fingers. And then, "Where everybody knows your name."

She stood up and reached through the hole, wrapping her other arm around Robert's neck impersonally, as if he were a piece of furniture.

"You'll have to help, Tosh," Robert muttered. "It's really awkward."

Tom put his arms around the girl's legs and hoisted her up. Her body felt soft and thick, but all the bulk came from layers of clothes. Underneath them, her body was as light and fragile as a bird's under its feathers.

As soon as her head was through the conservatory floor, she went rigid. Tom felt her legs stiffen, and she began to dart her head from side to side, making small whimpering noises.

"Out," he said quickly. "Shhh, shhh. Be quiet, please. Out."

The television was loud enough to stop her voice from being heard beyond the conservatory, but the whimpering sounds went on and on.

"What's upset her?" Tom hissed, frustrated because he couldn't see properly.

"I don't know. Let's get her out as fast as we can."

Robert hauled her up, almost roughly, and sat her on the edge of the hole, and Tom scrambled out behind her. She had a hand jammed over her mouth, but she was still whimpering. And each time she made a sound, she clenched her other hand into a loose fist and smacked it hard against her cheek.

"We can't do it," Robert said. "Look at her. We can't take her out of here."

"What are we supposed to do? Leave her?" Tom shook his head fiercely. "*We* didn't do this to her, Robbo. It's because she's been down in that hole. We've got to rescue her."

"But she can't understand. She's not—"

The girl's head was still going from side to side, peering around the dark conservatory. Suddenly, she put her hands to the ground and scuttled across to the television, on all fours. The moment its light hit her face, she relaxed and held her hands out toward it.

And suddenly Tom knew what she wanted. "Give me the flashlight, Robbo."

"But it's dangerous—"

"Hand it over." Tom clicked his fingers. "Don't you see? She's not used to being in the dark up here. This is the light place." He took the flashlight and turned it on, aiming it down at the floor, just in front of the television.

The girl froze, her eyes on the pool of light.

"Careful," Robert whispered. "Don't startle her."

Slowly, Tom moved the flashlight beam across the floor and up the front of the television. The girl's face was transformed. She stared at the moving light with an expression of wonder, as if it was the most beautiful thing she had ever seen.

"Well done," Robert muttered. "What happens if you try moving? Can we get her out of here?"

Step by step, Tom backed toward the door, circling the light in slow, regular loops. The girl followed him, still crawling, until he reached the door. Then he stopped, and she levered herself up onto her feet and began to move one hand around, imitating what he had been doing. She stood awkwardly, but she was quite steady.

After a moment or two, he started circling the flashlight again, and she copied him exactly, watching the patterns that the light made on the floor and mirroring his movements.

Without turning around, Tom reached behind him and opened the door. He stepped out backward, into the garden, and the girl whimpered again, holding her hands out to the flashlight.

"Shhh!" Tom said.

His voice was sharper than he meant it to be, because he was nervous. Immediately, her fist went up to her face, punching harder than before, so that she flinched sideways from her own blow.

"What are we going to do?" Robert whispered. "Maybe she's never been out. Maybe it's too frightening."

Tom took a few more steps backward, looping the flashlight around and around so that the beam made curlicues on the grass. The girl hovered in the doorway, with one hand held out toward him. He could see her whole body trembling. She wanted to come after him. There was no doubt about that. But she was obviously terrified.

He held out the flashlight, offering it to her, and she stretched out her hand to take it, but she was too far away. She gave a little moan and then jammed the other hand over her mouth again.

"Dohfuss," she muttered into it. To herself. "Dohfuss."

"I can't bear this," Robert said suddenly. "Let's just do it. Get out of the way, Tosh. I'm going to take her and go."

Without giving her any warning, he came up behind her and scooped her into his arms, going straight out through the conservatory door. She squirmed and pushed at his chest, but he was much stronger than she was.

"Shhh!" Tom said desperately. "Shhh!"

She was making louder noises now, but they were still stifled by her hand. Robert began moving toward the side gate, and Tom went to open it for him.

They were almost there when there was a small click, very loud in the silence. The kitchen door opened suddenly, and Warren was there, staring out at them.

"What are you doing?" he said.

2 4

FOR A SECOND THEY WERE ALL STILL, EXCEPT FOR THE GIRL, squirming in Robert's arms. The kitchen behind Warren was dark and empty, and he was hovering on the doorstep, gazing out at them in horror.

Then Robert said, "We're taking her away."

Warren shook his head frantically. "You can't," he whispered. "You mustn't."

"Don't worry," said Tom. "We'll make sure she's safe."

"You can't," Warren said again. "You've got to put her back." He came down the kitchen step, into the garden.

Robert backed toward the gate. "Don't try and stop us. Or we'll call the police."

Warren looked accusingly at Tom. "I thought you only wanted the computer and stuff. I never guessed you knew about Hope. You can't take her—my dad will kill me!"

He was still whispering, but his voice had risen. The girl put her head over Robert's shoulder and looked curiously at him.

"Wonn," she said. "Wonn. Dohfuss." And then she laughed. It was a weird, creaking noise. A laugh that went in instead of out, so that it was almost soundless.

"She's *ours*." Warren took another nervous step forward. "She'll die if you take her away. People won't understand what she's like."

"She'll die if she stays here," Robert said angrily. "No one can live in a hole in the ground."

"She's always lived there. It's her *room*." Warren was distraught. "If you take her away, the doctors will get her. They'll put her in a hospital and stick tubes into her body."

"*What?*" Robert stared at him.

Tom reached out and gave Robert a push, to keep him moving toward the gate. Then he turned back to Warren. "Did that happen before?" he said.

Warren hung his head. "Hope's *ours*," he repeated stubbornly. "And she's only safe when she's in her room. You have to put her back."

"It's not going to happen," Tom said gently. "No one's going to let you keep her down there. Not now that we know."

Warren scowled. "I'll call my dad—"

"I don't think you will."

Tom was pretty sure of that. It would have been the obvious thing to do, right at the beginning. But Warren hadn't done it—and that had to be because he was frightened. He thought all this was his fault. And in one sense, it was.

Tom hammered the point home, just to make sure. "If you call your dad, we'll tell him you let us in."

Robert took another step toward the gate, trying to sidle away without being noticed. But the girl whined and pushed at his chest to make him go back. For a moment, Tom thought she was complaining about leaving Warren.

Then he realized what she wanted. She was struggling to reach his flashlight. He put it into her hand, and, completely ignoring all of them, she began to wave it about, not wildly, but in regular, even loops. Her face was solemn and intent as she worked out the pattern.

Robert edged a little farther toward the gate.

Warren was terrified, shifting indecisively from one foot to the other. He obviously didn't know if he should follow Robert or call his father or stay where he was. Tom pressured him a bit more, to keep him where he was.

"You're out of your depth, Warren," he said. "You didn't choose to keep your sister in a hole, but no one's going to listen to that. Unless you let her go, there's going to be big trouble. And it'll hit you, too."

Warren made a small whimpering sound. "She's not used to being outside," he said. "She'll be cold. Bring her back in."

"We've thought of all that," Tom said. "We've brought clothes and a drink and something to eat. Don't worry. We'll look after her. Better than your dad does."

"Dad doesn't hurt her," Warren said. Pleading. Apologizing. "Not like—people you read about. He only wants to keep her safe for a little while. Until it's all right for her to come out."

Was that how it started? Just a little while. And then another little while. Week after week, year after year. Tom could imagine that. *Just a bit longer. We'll let her out soon—* until the secret was too dangerous to tell.

And the damage was too much to be cured.

"But how did it all begin?" he said, half to himself.

Warren shook his head, as if he'd never even thought of the question. From outside in the street, Tom could hear the soft sound of Robert's sneakers on the pavement. *Not much longer now. Just another few minutes.*

But he didn't get them. Suddenly, the light went on in the kitchen, and a voice said, "What are you doing, Warren? Who are you talking to?"

It was the woman. She came quickly through the kitchen and out into the garden, with her dressing gown clutched around her body. The moment she saw Tom, she looked sharply toward the conservatory—and saw the open door.

"Hope?" she said.

Tom didn't wait. Even before she had reached the conservatory, he bolted, not worrying about being careful or keeping quiet, but just covering the ground as quickly as he could. As he came through the gate, he could see Robert at the end of the street, still struggling to run with the girl in his arms.

Tom was going to shout a warning, but he didn't need to, because the noise from the garden hit first. There was a loud, open-throated yell, more frightening than any sound he'd ever heard. There were no words. The woman was screaming out of all control.

Robert had disappeared around the corner. Tom glanced over his shoulder and saw an upstairs light come on in the house behind him. Desperately he flung himself forward, trying to get out of sight before he was spotted. Frantically hoping that the man would head for the back of the house first, where the screaming was.

Please don't let him look out of the front window. Please let me get out of sight.

181

By the time he reached the corner, Robert and Emma had disappeared. There was nothing there except his own bike, leaning against a lamppost. But he could hear the girl's voice from somewhere across the road. She was screaming, too, but it was like the noise of her laugh, breathless and turned in on itself.

"Tom!" Emma called. "We're over here. Quick!"

She and Robert were standing between two houses, on a little pedestrian path that ran through from that road to the next one. Robert was trying to hold the girl on his bike, and Emma was ferreting in the bag they'd brought, looking for some way of distracting her. The flashlight was abandoned, rolling on the ground, and the girl was beating at Robert's chest with her fists.

Tom crossed the road quickly and pulled his bike back into the shadows. "Apple juice," he said quickly. "In the sports bottle." He picked up the flashlight and switched it off before it could give them away.

Emma pulled out the sports bottle and waved it in front of the girl, but she didn't seem to see it. In desperation, Emma pushed the top straight into the girl's open mouth—and, magically, she took it and began to suck, holding the bottle in one hand and twisting her matted hair with the other.

"Quick!" Robert muttered. He pushed the bike across the road, turning left and then right into the maze of little roads and pedestrian pathways. Tom and Emma followed him, turning off their lights and heading for the darkest side of the road.

They were around the first corner before they heard footsteps running down the street. They didn't look back. They just kept walking as hard as they could, turning left and right at random and gradually getting farther from the highway. Their sneakers were silent on the pavement, and the girl was still busy with the apple juice, sucking at the bottle as hard as she could.

Robert was struggling to hold her on his bike, and Tom and Emma were searching in the bag, hunting for something that would distract her when she'd finished the juice. They had turned left and right again before Tom found it.

He was just in time. The bottle was empty, and she was just taking it away from her mouth when he found what he wanted. He took it out and flapped it in front of her face.

It was a collection of pieces of wool knotted together at the top. There were ten of them, all different colors and thicknesses, and as he held them out, he flashed the flashlight on for a moment so that she could see what he was giving her.

She went very still when she saw what he was holding, but she didn't seem to want the light anymore. She flapped it away and reached for the wool, passing it through her hands over and over again. Then, as Tom switched off the flashlight, she began to make a new sound, quite different from anything he'd heard before. A faint, soft crooning, very low-pitched and contented. He had the curious idea that if he put a hand on her body, he would feel the noise vibrating through her, like purring through a cat.

She felt each strand carefully, ten or a dozen times, not looking down but staring blankly into the distance, as though all her attention was focused on her fingertips. Then her hand went up to her head, and she started picking through her hair.

Tom hadn't had a chance to look at it before. He'd just had a vague impression of long, irregular tangles, with things caught in them. Now he realized that each tangle was a neat braid. As they passed under the streetlights, he caught the flicker of different colors, wound in and out of the hair. A thread of blue. Red. A piece of thin gold ribbon.

The girl worked at one of the braids, pulling out a couple of strands. Then she lifted up the wool Tom had given her and began to wind it in and out of her hair, mixing the strands together. The pattern looked complicated and intricate, but her fingers were quick and deft, even though she couldn't see what she was doing.

"Look," Emma said softly. "She's making a twelve-strand braid. But it's not like yours, Rob. It's flat."

"I know," Robert muttered in an odd voice. "I could never manage that one." He tightened his arm around the girl's body to hold her steady on the bike. "Come on. Let's get out of here." He began to walk faster, turning left and right and right again as he hustled them down the hill.

"Don't you think we ought to go out to the main road?" Emma said. "It would be much quicker to go in a straight line."

Tom was just opening his mouth to agree when they heard a noise that made them stop dead.

Behind them, not very far away, a car had started. It was driving slowly through the development, turning left or right every few seconds.

25

"BANDO!" LORN CRAWLED THROUGH THE SECRET PASSAGE, calling his name. "Where are you? Come back!"

There was no answer. When she came out at the other end, she stood up in the darkness and called again.

"Bando? Are you there?" The sounds echoed in her ears, mapping out the space around her. There was no sign of Bando's huge, bulky figure, either to the left or to the right.

But she could smell him. His warm, distinctive scent hung faintly in the air to her left, and when she took a step in that direction, she could feel how his feet had roughened the earth of the floor. He had been moving quickly, running his hand along the side of the tunnel to keep some sense of where he was going.

Because he couldn't see. He thought he was following her, to save her from danger, but if anything happened, he would be helpless in the dark. For a second Lorn couldn't bear the thought of that. It was all her fault, and she was paralyzed with guilt.

She forced it to the back of her mind. Feeling guilty wouldn't help Bando now. What she had to do was think clearly so that she could find him as fast as possible. He'd gone off to the left, heading deeper into the earth. She had to go after him, even though she couldn't work out where he was or why he wasn't answering her calls.

As she started down the tunnel, her feet remembered the way. *Around this bend, the ground rises slightly. Then left and right, with stones on one side and roots hanging down loosely on the other* . . . Automatically, her mind registered all the little messages that built up the picture, but she was hardly aware of those. She was concentrating on the marks that Bando's feet had left and the way his scent grew stronger as she walked down the tunnel.

Then she picked up the strange slithering noise that she'd heard before. At first, it was nothing more than a disturbance in the air, a faint murmur coming through the earth. But it grew as she walked, swelling into a slow, slimy straining and gliding, like tentacles pulling at each other deep in the ground.

When she came to the place where the tunnel forked into two, she stopped and listened harder. The slithering was clear now, coming from the right-hand fork, and the air in there carried a new scent. Not the warm, rank animal smell that had been with her all the way, but a fleshy, rancid tang, coming down the tunnel in waves as the noises swelled and faded.

Oh, Bando, you didn't go that way, did you? Please, please . . .

But she knew he had. The bare soles of her feet could feel his footprints leading directly into the right-hand tunnel.

She followed them, shivering as the chill settled into her bones. This was new territory. She should have been clicking her tongue and listening to the shape of the ground, but she was afraid to make any noise of her own, so she felt her way blindly, fumbling at the walls. Once or twice, her fingers slipped into the wide, clumsy dents that Bando had left when he went through before her.

Where was he? Why couldn't she hear him?

The slithering sounds were even louder now. Her mind built them into nightmare patterns, visualizing monstrous, ridged tentacles that writhed against each other. Their tips twisted grotesquely, brushing at the earth, and their long shapes gathered inward, into a mass that was too intricate for her to picture from the sounds.

Was that where Bando was, trapped in the center?

The creature was ten or twenty times her size. It was very close, but she had no sense of warmth from its body. That must mean that it was cold—like the wet, heavy earth around it. She had never heard of anything like that, not even in Zak's wildest stories. All her instincts told her to turn and run.

But she couldn't. She had to find Bando.

She began to walk forward, creeping carefully now. Her senses told her that the creature was near, around the next bend in the tunnel. But it was occupied with its own movements and she was very small. If she slipped around quietly, maybe it wouldn't notice her. Maybe she would have time to figure out what it was and whether Bando was really there. Her feet padded silently over the soft earth, going slowly, slowly around the bend, until she found—

Nothing.

The tunnel was empty.

At first, she didn't believe it. She went from one side to the other, stretching out her arms to feel the space. But her first reaction was right. There was nothing in the tunnel, even though the noise of the monster was everywhere, filling her ear and shaking the air around her.

It took her a second to realize that it was coming from over her head.

When she understood, she threw herself at the nearest wall, digging her fingers in so that she could claw her way up. As she went, her hand closed around a stone, and she worked it loose and took it with her, until she was as high as she could climb, with her head jammed up against the roof of the tunnel. Then she began to scrape away the earth above her, clinging on with one hand and stabbing the stone in with the other.

The first ten or dozen strokes were difficult. Then, without warning, the roof gave way, as though she had broken through some kind of crust. Loose earth began to fall all around her, and she turned her head away to keep it out of her eyes.

As she moved, something wet and heavy slapped against her cheek.

The shock broke her grip on the wall, and she went tumbling down in a rain of earth and stones, with her mind bombarded by images of another time and another place.

She knew them, she knew that slap against her cheek— the feel of cold, slimy flesh—hands that grabbed at her, wrenching her out into dazzling light—and words that stabbed at her ears.

That's filthy! Look—in her hair. It's disgusting!
She's plaited them in!
Get the scissors! Quick!

The pattern moves by itself, making new shapes and
slithering against the cheek and the neck and the ears, and
it's beautiful—but they're cutting it all away, and it's bad,
bad, BAD—

It was there in her mind, real and sharp. All she had to do was concentrate, and she would remember, like the others. She would *understand—*

But she couldn't do it. Not now. Because Bando was more important than that. She couldn't think about anything except finding him.

Still falling, she wrenched herself back to *now* and *here.* High above her head, there was a small new opening where the earth had fallen away. It let in a few weak glimmers of moonlight, and she looked up to see what had slapped against her face.

It was falling with her. She twisted in the air, just in time to avoid the full weight of its clammy, stinking flesh as they hit the ground together. The light caught the ridges on its long, writhing body and gleamed dull on the gray-pink skin. Its smell caught at the back of her nose.

And it wasn't one monstrous creature, but dozens of ordinary ones. Earthsnakes, tied together in a cruel knot. Their bodies moved in aimless, irregular spasms, and their stink filled the small space where she was lying. They were ugly and unpleasant, but there was no harm in them.

For a second she relaxed, ready to laugh at herself for taking so long to understand. Then one of the earthsnakes twisted up toward her—and she saw that it had no head. It was still alive, but instead of narrowing to a point, its body ended abruptly, in revolting, ragged shreds.

Some other creature had bitten through the naked flesh, leaving it helpless and unable to escape.

Sitting up, Lorn peered through the gloom, letting her eyes travel from one earthsnake to another. They were all the same. Something had wound them into a tangled ball and then bitten off their heads, leaving them buried in the ground like a store of living meat.

She had no idea what kind of monster did that. All she knew was that it was loose in the tunnels.

Dragging herself off the ground, she began to feel around on the earth with her feet. It was impossible to smell anything except the raw stench of the earthsnakes, but it didn't take her long to find one of Bando's big, untidy footprints. And then another. And another.

He was still ahead of her, going on down the tunnel. She had no idea how much farther he'd gone, but she knew she had to reach him, before the monster did.

Ignoring the stink of the earthsnakes, she took a long breath of air. And then she started to run.

26

THE CAR'S ENGINE SOUNDED LOUD AND THREATENING IN the darkness. They stood between the houses, trying to work out which way it was going as it crawled from one road to another. It seemed to be turning left and right at random.

Then it turned again—and Tom understood. There was nothing random about the turns. The car was moving systematically outward from the Armstrongs' street, methodically covering the whole development. And the driver knew the roads much better than they did.

"It's tracking us down," he muttered. "Figuring out where we are."

Robert shook his head grimly, and Emma caught her breath—stifling the noise with her hand. The girl was the only one who didn't react. If she understood what Tom had said, she didn't show any sign of it. She went on twisting the wool into her hair, with her eyes half closed and her face intent on the complicated pattern she was making.

"We'll have to take the footpaths," Emma whispered. "It's our only chance."

The car turned again, coming nearer, and Robert heaved the girl up in his arms, shifting her weight from one arm to the other.

"I can't carry her much farther," he said. "Can we put her on a bike? We could go faster then."

"She'll make a noise," Emma said doubtfully.

"It's the only hope we've got." Robert's voice was firm. "Hold my bike while I have a go."

At first, they thought it was going to be easy. The girl didn't seem to notice when Robert rested her body on the seat. But when he tried to move one arm, to hold the handlebars, she looked up sharply and started to squeal in a small, shrill voice.

"We can't do it," Emma said. "She's terrified. She—"

And then the car turned onto the road where they were standing.

Its headlights were full on, lighting up the tarmac and both sidewalks, all the way down the road, and it was coming straight toward them. Robert tightened his arms around the girl and lifted her off the bike again.

"Shhh," he whispered. "Please. Be quiet." His voice was gentle, but he sounded anxious and urgent, and she cowered away from him.

"Quiet. Quiet," she mumbled, shaking her head from side to side. "Stupid. Dohfuss." One hand went over her mouth, and the other one started punching at the side of her head.

There's something wrong with her, Tom thought. *What are we going to do?* Because they couldn't let her go back. Not ever. Not to that horrible hole under the floor.

Emma was concentrating on more practical things. "No one's going to see us here. Not if we stay back between the houses. We can just wait for the car to go past."

"No, we can't," Robert said. "Look." He nodded at the road.

As the car came toward them, someone inside was shining a flashlight from side to side, now on the left and now on the right, lighting up every house and every front garden. And every gap between the houses.

"They're bound to see us if we stay here," Robert said.

"But where can we go?" Emma's voice was panicky now. "There's nowhere else to hide."

"Yes, there is." Without hesitating, Robert unlatched the gate behind him. "We can get in here. Hurry up." Still carrying the girl, he went straight through, into the small garden behind the house.

"We can't go in there," Emma muttered.

"Of course we can." Tom pushed her, hard. "Quick—before the car gets here."

Somehow, he got her through and lugged the bikes behind him. As he pulled the gate shut, Robert hissed from near his ankles.

"Get down. As fast as you can. Otherwise they'll see us over the gate."

Emma flopped onto the concrete, and Tom crouched as low as he could, letting the bikes fall sideways against him. They were just in time. A second later, the flashlight beam swept across the gate. It shone through the lattice panel at the top, showing the diamond pattern, and the girl gave a small gurgle of pleasure.

"Quiet," Tom murmured.

And then wished he hadn't, as she hit herself again.

They waited until the car had gone all the way up the road and turned left. Then they struggled onto their feet. Tom could see that Robert's strength was running out. It took him a lot of effort to heave the girl off the ground, and he was breathing hard as he stood up.

"Let's try the bike again," Tom whispered.

Robert shook his head. "No chance. We can't risk being seen on the roads. We'll have to leave the bikes here and go through the back gardens. Maybe she'll walk a bit if we do that. Otherwise we'll have to take turns carrying her."

"Leave our *bikes*?" Emma's voice was too loud for comfort. "But we can't just abandon them."

"Depends what you think is important." Robert shrugged. "Ride yours home if you like. I'm going this way." He set off down the garden, hoisting the girl higher so that she rested against his shoulder.

"He's mad," Emma said. "Completely mad. We can't—"

"Shhh," Tom said softly. "It's her or the bikes. Did you really expect him to choose the bikes? How about you?"

"I'm following Rob, of course," Emma said wearily. "But I don't know what Mom and Dad are going to say about the bikes."

"I can come back and get them tomorrow," Tom said soothingly.

He wasn't sure it was true. He couldn't imagine what would be happening by tomorrow. But he wheeled the bikes down the garden and pushed them behind a shed, hiding them as well as he could. Then he and Emma went to help Robert.

Getting over into the next garden was easier than he'd expected. There was a garbage can in the far corner, hidden behind a trellis. He used it to help himself over the fence, and then Emma climbed up and sat on top of it, reaching down for the girl so that she could lift her over to Tom.

"She's wet," she whispered as she took Hope onto her lap.

She was very wet, Tom realized when she came down into his arms. And cold. And shaking. And she was very, very frightened. As he lowered her down, her fingers moved faster and faster through her hair, not using the wool now—that was already finished—but braiding new strands that she had pulled out of old braids. He could feel her tugging hard at them, as if she wanted to hurt herself.

"Where are the clothes you brought?" he whispered to Emma as soon as she was over the fence. "We've got to get her warm."

Emma took them out of her backpack, and they pulled them on. It was hard to get the girl's hands free long enough to push her arms into the sleeves. Her whole body was tense with fear, and her fingers were locked in her hair. It took all three of them to wrestle her into a sweater and warm jacket, and the moment she was in them, she went back to her twisting, twisting, twisting.

Then they tried to get her to walk down the garden, but that was hopeless. She could stand, but she wouldn't walk. When Tom and Robert tried to pull her along, she bent her knees so that she was swinging between the two boys. In the end, Tom and Emma carried her between them, to give Robert a rest. Her body felt small and slight, but by the time they came out into the light at the front of the house, Tom's arms were starting to ache.

He and Emma kept the girl in the shadows while Robert went ahead, across the road. They could hear the car some-where off to the right, but when it turned, it turned away from them. Robert scouted along a little way and then came back and beckoned.

"We can get through easily down there. Let's go."

It was worse than any journey Tom had ever imagined. He lost count of the number of gardens they crossed. Once there was a security light, and they had to bolt to the far end before anyone woke up. Three times they found themselves in gardens with high, flimsy fences that were impossible to climb, and they had to backtrack and look for another way. And all the time the car was circling around and around, waiting for a chance to catch them on the road. Waiting for them to make a mistake.

They were seen twice.

Once, they were just running across a road, and the car turned in at the other end. As they plunged into the darkness on the far side, they heard it speed up, heading toward them. But it was too far away to see exactly where they went. And they didn't wait to be found. They streaked down the side of the nearest house and went straight over the fence at the bottom of that garden, into the next one.

"Stop here," Robert breathed. "Try and figure out what they're doing."

They crouched behind a clump of bushes and listened. The car had stopped, and they heard someone coming slowly down the road, calling in a deep voice. After a couple of minutes, they saw a flashlight beam in the garden they had just left. It shined right down to the bottom fence, and the voice called softly from up by the house.

"Hope? Are you there? Can you hear me?"

It was Mr. Armstrong. In the garden on the other side of the fence.

The girl's head came up and she looked around quickly. Tom thought she was going to answer, but Robert laid a hand lightly over her mouth, and she slumped back against his chest. Tom held his breath until the light moved away again and they heard Mr. Armstrong calling by the next house. Then they darted down the garden, away from him, and across the next road.

The second time they were nearly caught was when they had reached the very far side of the development. They hadn't heard the car for a long time, and exhaustion made them careless. They came out opposite a big, twenty-four-hour supermarket, and Emma pointed at the line of shopping carts halfway up the parking lot.

"We could borrow one of those," she said.

The girl was asleep by then, hunched against Robert's shoulder. They had all carried her farther than they could ever have imagined, and the shopping carts looked like the most beautiful things in the world.

"Brilliant!" Tom said. "Let's go."

They crept across the road and into the parking lot. There were about half a dozen cars parked close to the store. Apart from those, the whole place was deserted, but the lot was brightly lit. Tom maneuvered a cart out of the bay, and Robert lowered the girl gently into it, trying not to wake her.

All they had to do now was go through the pedestrian area in the middle of the city and down the slope on the other side. That would take them to the back of the park and into the little woods.

If they hadn't been so tired, they would have gone around the edge of the parking lot, staying in the shadows. But they were so tired now that every extra step seemed like a huge burden. So they headed straight across the lot.

And Mr. Armstrong's car came suddenly up the hill from the development, on the main road to their right. He saw them. There was no doubt about that. The brakes squealed, and the car turned suddenly left, heading for the supermarket entrance.

"Run!" said Emma.

And they ran.

27

We'll take her straight into the woods, ROBERT HAD SAID when they were making their plans. *And then we'll try and contact Lorn.* But how could they do that with Mr. Armstrong after them? If they stopped, they'd be caught.

They pelted through the pedestrian mall at top speed, with the cart bumping along and swerving around corners. Tom was pushing it, and whenever they went through a patch of light, he could see the girl huddled up in the bottom, with her eyes wide open. One hand was twirling her hair, and the other was around the bars of the cart, gripping them tightly.

Someone was coming after them. But it didn't sound like Mr. Armstrong. It was someone lighter and quicker. *So Mr. Armstrong's still driving the car*, Tom thought. *He could be coming around the other way to cut us off.*

Robert had realized that, too. As they reached the end of the mall, he bent over to mutter to Tom. "We've got to split up. You and Emma go on with the cart, and I'll take her and go a different way."

"But won't they notice you're missing?"

"Not if we can get to the park before they do. Use the flashlight a bit, to keep them following." Robert bent over the cart and put his arms around the girl's tense, frightened body. "Come on, you," he said.

"Hope," said Tom.

"What?" Robert looked up.

"Her name's Hope," Tom said. "Not *You*."

Robert shook his head and hauled the girl out of the cart. "Just run, Tosh. Don't waste time fussing."

"Dohfuss. Dohfuss," the girl said lightly. She leaned sideways against Robert and closed her eyes. Her face was pale and she looked very tired.

"Take her home, Rob," Emma said. "Then you'll have Mom and Dad if you need them."

"*Run!*" Robert stepped back into the shadows and nodded them on.

Emma took off her backpack and dumped it into the cart. Then she and Tom shot out of the pedestrian mall. The empty cart rattled and jumped, and its wheels sounded loud and hard on the pavement. Out of the corner of his eye, Tom saw Mr. Armstrong's car coming along the side of the square, not quite near enough to stop them.

"Let's give him a run for his money," he yelled.

They raced down the slope and around the corner. The big, ornamental park gates were locked at dusk, but that was just for show. There was no fence along the side of the park to keep people out at night. Just a hedge with lots of openings, and the woods at the far end. As soon as they were past the gates, Tom swerved left, off the pavement and into the trees.

He heard the car brake fiercely behind them.

"That's one," Emma panted. "At least."

They were heading straight down the park, toward the woods. When they were halfway there, Tom glanced back over his shoulder and saw Mr. Armstrong coming after them. He moved in a strange, lumbering way, but it was faster than Tom would have expected. And he hadn't been running for nearly as long as they had. Emma was starting to fail now. Tom could hear her breath coming in great tearing gasps, and she had one hand pressed against her side.

"Not far now," he said, raising his voice above the rattle of the cart. "Keep it up, Em."

Emma made a last, heroic effort, and they reached the end of the park and went through the hedge, into the woods. After that, it was easy. There were dozens and dozens of little, twisting paths, and Tom knew every one of them. Every patch of brambles and every muddy ditch. He'd pulled Helga out of all of them at least once.

He found the driest ditch for Emma and left her there with a clump of dead bracken trampled across to cover her. Then he enjoyed himself rattling up and down the paths, well away from anything important like Emma and the hedge bank.

Once or twice Mr. Armstrong tried to cut across and head him off, but his feet were heavy and clumsy, and he was starting to breathe hard. Tom just grinned to himself and changed direction. There was no way that anything like that was going to work in these woods. This was *his* maze.

When it began to get boring—and Robert had had enough time to reach home safely—Tom worked his way gradually to the very edge of the woods. Lifting Emma's backpack onto his shoulder, he stepped out onto the pavement and gave the cart one last, huge push.

It rattled down the road, and he ducked sideways into a clump of rhododendrons, watching Mr. Armstrong charge past him and run after it. It didn't take him more than a few moments to realize that he had been tricked. He turned around and began to walk back along the pavement.

As he passed the bushes where Tom was hiding, the light from a streetlamp caught his face full on. It was still completely without expression. He didn't even look out of breath. Only his eyes moved, looking left and right as he went. Deep in the rhododendrons, Tom shuddered and kept very still.

A few moments later, he heard the car drive away. But he waited for a good quarter of an hour after that, just to be sure that it wasn't some kind of trap. Then he slipped out of the bushes and went to find Emma.

She was lying exactly where he had left her, very still and quiet. But he must have been even quieter. As he padded up to the ditch, he heard a faint, stifled sniff.

"If you make noises like that, someone's going to come and catch you," he said. "What's the matter?"

She sat up fiercely. "I'm fine!" she said. And then sniffed again.

Tom sat down on the edge of the ditch. "What's up?" he said. "Were you scared?"

"Of course not." Emma could still manage a touch of scorn. "What could he do to *us*? We can call the police if things get really tough. But that girl—"

Tom didn't need it spelled out for him. "Maybe she'll get better. Now that she's out of that hole."

"Maybe," Emma said. But she didn't sound convinced. She scrambled out of the ditch and started brushing bracken off her clothes. "I'm absolutely freezing."

"You'd better make yourself a cup of coffee when you get home."

"Are you joking?" Emma said. "Mom would be downstairs as soon as I turned on the pot. She's a really light sleeper. It took us hours to get out of the house tonight without waking her."

"I'll make you a drink on the way home then. My mom sleeps as if she's hibernating." Tom didn't really expect her to say yes, but she nodded briskly.

"That's great. Now let's get out of here."

WHEN THEY WERE THERE, SITTING IN THE KITCHEN, TOM realized that she was deliberately wasting time. She drank her coffee as slowly as she could, cupping her hands around the mug and peering into it. And when Helga came nosing around her ankles, she stopped drinking and bent down to pat her head and talk to her.

Anything to avoid going home.

"It's no use," Tom said at last. "You've got to be back before your mom wakes up."

"I know." Emma looked up and gave him a rueful grin. "But nothing's ever going to be the same, is it? Whatever happens."

"I guess not." Tom picked up his jacket. "Come on. I'll walk you back." Helga perked up her ears and wagged her tail, and he shook his head at her. "Not you, silly dog."

But he should have known that that wasn't good enough. Not when it was almost morning and she was expecting a walk anyway. She wagged her tail and gave a short, high-pitched bark.

"Shhh." Tom put a finger to his lips. "Even Mom wakes up if there's barking."

But Helga just barked again, sounding slightly injured, and he saw that they would have to take her if they wanted her to be quiet. He clipped on her leash and opened the back door.

Outside, it was still dark, but there was slightly more traffic about. They walked quickly past the park and across the road to Robert and Emma's house.

"Come in," Emma said quickly. "Just till we see what's happened to *her*."

"To Hope?" Tom said.

Emma nodded and unlatched the back gate.

As she pushed it open, Robert appeared suddenly, whispering through the dark. "Where have you been? I thought you were never coming."

"What have you done with Hope?" Tom whispered back. "Is she in the house?"

Robert shook his head. "I couldn't risk her waking Mom. She's in there." He pointed at the little shed where he and Emma kept their bicycles.

"Is she all right?" Tom said quickly.

"Of course she is," Robert muttered. "As all right as she'll ever be." He went over and pushed the shed door open. "Where's the flashlight? Take a look at her."

Hope was huddled in the corner, fast asleep in a pile of blankets. She had a banana in one hand, half-eaten, and her face was smeared with squashed banana pulp. All the plaits on her head were twisted together into one matted mess, and her wet clothes were starting to smell. Helga pushed her head around Tom's legs and sniffed curiously at the air inside the shed.

Looking down at Hope, Tom was suddenly so angry that he could hardly speak. Because he knew she couldn't ever recover from what had been done to her. Not in the normal course of things. She would never be all right unless this loopy idea of Robert's worked.

So it had to.

"When are we going to take her across to the park?" he said. "Any reason why we shouldn't go now?"

There was an odd, unaccountable pause. Then Robert said, "I don't think we ought to do that." His voice was tight and miserable. "I'm going to phone the police and hand her over."

"*What?*" said Emma.

Tom was stunned. "So why did we go through all that performance tonight? We could have made a phone call in the first place. You were the one who insisted on doing it the hard way—because you said she was Lorn. Are you telling me that's all nonsense?"

"Oh no," Robert said. "It's not nonsense. She's Lorn all right. I knew it as soon as I saw her winding that string into her hair."

There was no mistaking the misery now. He sounded utterly wretched. Hope stirred and turned her head, wiping banana into her hair, and Robert's face twisted as if he couldn't bear to see it.

"So why have you changed your mind?" Tom was very

angry now. If he'd known what to do, he would have scooped Hope up and taken her to the park himself. "What's different?"

"Suppose we take her to the park," Robert said slowly, "and she—and the same thing happens that happened to me. Suppose she and Lorn go back to being one person."

"I thought that was the point." Tom glanced at Emma, wondering if he'd missed something. But she was looking baffled, too. "I thought that was what you wanted. One person."

"Only if it's Lorn!" Robert said fiercely. "But we don't *know*, do we? Suppose it isn't Lorn. Suppose it's her. Hope. She won't be any better off then, will she? And Lorn will be gone. Vanished. *She won't exist anywhere.* I'll really have lost her then. How can I risk that?"

Tom was looking at Hope again. At her pale skin and her matted hair and the fine—too fine—bones of her head. There was a bruise on her right cheek, in the place where her fist landed when she punished herself for making a noise, and the palms of her hands were dark with ingrained dirt.

"You can't *not* risk it," he said. Just as fiercely as Robert.

28

As Lorn ran down the tunnel, the reek of the earthsnakes faded gradually. When she picked up Bando's scent again, it was stronger, but there was something else, too. A sweet, rotting smell that she didn't understand.

She called his name, hoping he was close enough to hear. "Bando?"

There was no answer. And there was something strange about the sound of her voice. The space ahead seemed . . . too big. Cautiously she called again.

"Bando? Are you there?"

The words dropped away into emptiness.

What was ahead of her? Some kind of cavern? Her mind tried out the picture and rejected it. There was space, but not like that. It sounded more as though the floor in front of her was about to disappear. She went down on her hands and knees and began to crawl forward carefully.

That was what saved her from falling. Her hands went down once, twice, three times—and then they skidded on loose earth and stones and slid from underneath her. She sprawled flat on her front, hearing the stones she had dislodged go tumbling down and down into—what?

It was very deep. The stones landed with a slow, soft *pfff,* and a breath of warm air came floating up toward her. For a moment she was terrified, thinking that she had found the monstrous animal from the tunnels, asleep in its den.

Then she began to decode the rich mixture of scents that the air brought with it. The smell of the animal was certainly there—as it was everywhere around her—but with it came the sweet scent she had noticed before. This time she recognized it—and understood.

The heat came from the plants that carpeted the den. The whole deep, rounded space was lined with decomposing leaves and moss, generating heat as they rotted. When she stretched her hands down, she could feel the plants' soft, decaying fibers. They had been put there deliberately, and worked into a thick layer that covered the floor and walls of the den.

She could only reach the very top of the layer, and the floor was far, far below. The ground fell away almost vertically, and she hung over the edge, listening and breathing and turning her face to the air. Trying to figure out what was down at the bottom of the hole.

Bando's scent was part of the complicated mix of smells that drifted up toward her. And there was a faint sound of breathing coming from way down at the bottom of the hole. She called out again, just loud enough to carry.

"Bando?"

The rhythm of the breathing faltered, and there was a faint, muffled grunt. It barely reached her, but she knew what it was. She had heard it a hundred times in the cavern, and she would have known it anywhere. Bando was down below her, in the monster's den.

"What's the matter?" she hissed. "Are you hurt?"

This time there was no response, not even a grunt. That meant he was unconscious—or worse. He must have gone charging over the edge of the den, without even realizing it was there. And then—what? Had he been hit by a stone as he fell?

Lorn didn't know, but she knew he was in appalling danger. And it was her fault. If he came around, he would be terrified, and she hated the idea that he might find himself alone. Her first instinct was to slide straight down the steep slope in front of her, to get to him as fast as she could.

But that was stupid. If she did that, they would both be trapped. If they tried to climb out of the hole, the rotting plants would just give way under their fingers. And if Bando was unconscious, she wouldn't be able to lift him.

She had to go back. To get help.

Turning away from the den was the hardest thing she had ever done. But she had to do it. Without that, Bando had no chance at all. Hauling herself to her feet, she began to run back along the tunnel as fast as she could.

SHE WENT THROUGH THE SECRET PASSAGE AND OUT INTO the storeroom, without pausing for a second. She was breathless from running and covered with slime from squeezing back past the earthsnakes, but she knew exactly what she was going to do next.

And she knew who could make it work, without asking endless questions.

Thank goodness for Cam, she thought as she snatched a coil of rope from the stack in the corner. *Thank goodness she's back*.

She raced straight up the ramp, but she slowed down as she went around the brazier into the cavern. She didn't want the others to wake up. The more people she had to speak to, the slower she would be getting back to Bando. Only Cam needed to hear.

Cam was sitting on the other side of the brazier, in a warm corner. As Lorn came into the cavern, Cam looked sharply at her. But she didn't say anything. Not until Lorn slipped across and knelt beside her.

Then she raised her eyebrows. "So what's up?"

"I've done something terrible," Lorn said softly. "Bando's in danger, and I have to get back to him as fast as I can. But I can't get him out without some others to help. Can you send them after me?"

"Where?" Cam said. Short and efficient.

"Tell them to come down the ramp and then follow the rope." Lorn patted the coil looped over her shoulder. "I'll leave a trail for them."

"How many people?"

"Five. Tell them to bring blades—and to keep their ears open. And to go straight past the earthsnakes."

Cam raised her eyebrows again, but she didn't waste time on nonessential talk. She just nodded briskly. "Be quick," she said. "And careful."

Lorn nodded back. "Thanks." And then, "I'm sorry."

"That's for later," Cam said. "Now get out of the way before I tell the others."

As Lorn headed back toward the storeroom, she heard Cam start to call the others together. *You can always trust Cam*, she thought. Then she slipped around the brazier and ran down the ramp, pausing at the bottom to knot one end of her rope around the end of a root.

She paid it out across the storeroom, catching up more coils as she passed the rope store. Then she was back in the secret passage, pushing the ropes ahead of her as she wriggled through.

She knew the others wouldn't be far behind her, but she couldn't wait for them. She had to get back to Bando. Before anything else happened to him.

2 9

"WE'VE GOT TO DO IT!" TOM SAID AGAIN. "WE'VE GOT TO take her across to the park!"

He said it more fiercely this time, trying to push Robert into agreeing. It had always worked before when things were difficult. They might argue, but if he tried hard enough, he'd always been able to get Robert to give in. In the end.

Not this time, though. Robert just stood where he was, blocking the doorway and looking miserable and determined. "We don't know what we're dealing with," he said stubbornly. "It's stupid to rush in and start meddling. We need to understand more."

Helga whined and pulled at her leash, looking up at Tom. He patted her head to reassure her, but she could feel his agitation, and she whined again.

"You'll never understand if you don't *do* anything," Emma said. "I thought that was why you were so eager to track her down. So you could find out a bit more, and figure out what happened to you. You'll never get another chance like this."

"Who cares about that?" Tom said impatiently. "The important thing is that *she'll* never get another chance. If we let her down now, other people will whisk her away, and she'll be like this forever."

He looked down at the girl on the floor of the shed.

Because her eyes were closed, he'd been assuming that she was fast asleep, but now he saw that she was listening hard. Her ear was cocked toward them, catching every sound.

"Hope?" he said softly. "Can you hear us? Open your eyes."

Her eyelids flickered and then opened a crack. Warily, she turned her head toward them, and her eyes moved slowly along the floor. When they reached Helga, they stopped for a long time. Helga wagged her tail and barked once, but it was a subdued bark. She sounded cautious and uncertain.

When the girl heard the bark, she lay very still for a moment, sniffing at the air. Tom let his hand rest lightly on Helga's head to calm her down.

"Easy," he said under his breath. "Easy, Helga."

Slowly, the girl sat up, lifting her head so that she was looking straight at Tom. For the first time, he met her eyes directly. But there was no sense of communication. He might as well have been part of the shed. It was impossible to tell how he looked to her, or whether she could make any sense of their rush through the night and the bare wooden floor where she was lying now.

He wanted to talk to her, to speak and hear her answer. And he wanted Robert to hear it, too, so that he understood that this girl was just as real as the other one under the ground. But how could you talk to someone who looked at you as if you were a piece of wood?

He took a step closer to her, keeping Helga's leash very short. "Hope," he said gently. And then, "Is that your name?"

A small frown drifted across her face, as if she were thinking about a puzzle. "Where everybody," she said, rolling her tongue around her mouth. "Where everybody knows."

"Your name?" Tom said. "Where everybody knows your name?"

This time, her smile was brilliant, transforming her whole face. But it wasn't a smile for Tom. It was as though she didn't understand that he was watching her. She was like someone smiling in the dark. The smile flooded over her face and vanished without lingering.

A moment later, she was bending over the blankets wrapped around her, working at the fringed ends with her fingers and frowning as she concentrated. Tom watched her for a moment, trying to pick up the pattern she was making. Red over blue. Brown under red. Blue over blue over blue. It was too intricate for him to follow, but he could see that it was neat and regular, interweaving the fringes so that all three blankets were joined together.

"What are we going to do with her then?" Emma said. "Hand her over to social services? Call the police?"

"We're taking her to the park," Tom said again. "That's what we've got to do, if she's really Lorn. And she is, isn't she?" He glanced up sharply.

"She *looks* like Lorn," Robert muttered. "The way Lorn would look if she'd been kept in a hole for years. And her voice is the same—or it would be, if she didn't do that weird thing with her tongue. But that's not how Lorn *is*. She's—"

Tom didn't wait for him to finish. "Lorn's the way Hope *ought* to be," he said fiercely. "That's it, isn't it? But Hope's had that stolen away. And this might be her only chance to get it back. Even if nothing happens in the park, we've got to *try*!"

Robert was wavering. Tom could see it. It would take only another little push, one final argument. But what was left to say? What could make the difference?

It was Emma who found it. She had been staring down at Hope, watching her hands move over the fringes. Suddenly, she said, "Why didn't Lorn go with you on that journey? When you came home across the park. Did you ask her to come?"

"Of course I asked her," Robert said. "But she wouldn't come. She wouldn't take the risk."

"And do you wish she had?" Emma said it without looking at him. Still staring at Hope's quick, clever fingers.

Robert didn't answer for a moment. Then he stepped sideways, away from the door. "OK," he muttered. "We'll take her to the park."

THEY HAD TO TAKE ALL THE BLANKETS, TOO. WHEN THEY tried to unwrap her, her eyes widened in panic, and she started to make small, painful noises, clinging onto the blankets with one hand and hitting at her face with the other. Tom couldn't bear to watch.

"Let her have them," he said. "What difference does it make? We have to get over there."

They wound her into the blankets, as tightly as they could, and Robert bent down and heaved her off the floor. Tom saw her shrink back, almost imperceptibly, as he touched her, and he wondered if she understood more than she could say.

When they stepped outside the shed, they realized that it was almost morning. It was still dark, but there was a faint, gray lightening in the sky over the city center. As Robert carried Hope through the front garden and onto the pavement, her head lifted and she glanced from side to side, looking wary and perplexed. Tom saw her sniff at the cold air and turn her face up to catch it against her skin, but he couldn't tell whether she was enjoying herself or watching fearfully for some new kind of danger.

Robert glanced quickly left and right, crossed the road, and turned along the front of the park, past the big, locked gates. It was too early to get in that way. They would have to go around the corner and in through the first gap in the hedge.

Tom was close behind him, with Helga trotting at his heels, bright and excited. No use trying to tell her that this was just her usual early morning walk. She knew it was something special, and she was up for any adventure. Tom suddenly realized that it was probably not a good idea to take her into the woods. He'd have to tie her up before they got there. And she wasn't going to like that.

"Sorry," he said as they went around the corner. "You'll just have to be—"

He didn't finish, because he had a sudden glimpse of a long, gray car driving away from them, down the side of the park. His heart thumped, hard.

"What's the matter?" Emma said quickly.

"I just—" He was going to tell her. But before he could get the words out, he thought, *What will Robert say? Will it make him turn back?* So he mumbled something about Helga and let it go.

Anyway, it couldn't really have been the same car. He was just being paranoid. Mr. Armstrong must have given up and gone home long ago.

It was frosty in the park, and they were the only people there. The grass crunched under their feet, and they left long, clear trails behind them as they walked down toward the woods. Hope let go of her braiding for a second and rubbed at her nose with the palm of her hand.

"Yes," Tom said. "It's cold. That's frost on the ground."

She didn't give any sign that she'd heard him, but a moment later, he heard her muttering the word into her blankets. *Fross, fross, frosssssssss* . . . She had finished the braiding by then and pulled herself down inside her wrappings, so that only the top half of her head was visible. When Robert shifted her weight across his body, she made a tiny protesting noise and wriggled around so that she could still see where they were going.

When they reached the hedge at the bottom of the park, Tom looked for a place where he could leave Helga.

"Sorry," he said as he tied her leash to the leg of a bench. "The woods are not a good place for dogs just now. You'll have to stay and keep guard." She gazed up at him, whining and straining at her leash, and he said it again, very clearly, so that she knew exactly what he meant. "Stay, Helga. Stay."

The others were already in the woods. When he followed them through the hedge, he saw them picking their way carefully along the side of the overgrown ditch. Hope had turned around now, and she was looking over Robert's shoulder.

"Hi," Tom said. "Here I am again."

He gave her a grin, wondering if she had been looking for him. Willing her to respond. For a second he thought there was . . . something. Then she turned around, to see what was ahead.

It was only a few days since Tom had last walked along the back of the hedge bank, but it was already different. The green plants had a sickly, winter look, and the dead ones had been beaten down by rain and trampling feet. He couldn't tell anymore how to find the cavern entrance.

But Robert didn't hesitate. He stopped just before it and knelt, lowering Hope onto the ground. Then he pulled a little white paper bag out of his pocket.

"Oh well done," Emma said. "You've brought them something to eat."

"Not really. Just a few nuts." He tipped them into the palm of his hand, and something else fell out, too. A tiny roll of fine, white cloth, like a strip cut from a handkerchief. "But I've made this banner. I did it yesterday."

He unrolled it so that they could see. The ends were glued to matchsticks, to make it easy to handle, and in between the wooden ends were three words, written in black ink.

COME OUT LORN.

"Can she read?" Emma said tentatively.

"How should I know? But maybe someone can. Anyway, it was the only thing I could think of."

Robert tipped the nuts onto his lap so that he could use

both hands to roll the banner up again. Hope's hand darted out of the blankets and snatched up one of the nuts.

"No," Emma said. "They're not for you, Hope."

She reached out to take the nut back, and Hope clutched it tightly, turning away from them all.

"Let her alone," Robert said. "We don't want a fuss. And it's only one nut." He finished rolling the banner and put it back into the bag with the rest of the nuts. Then he stretched up and snapped a twig from the hedge. "Let's see what happens, then."

He began to push the stick carefully into the little tunnel in front of them, and Emma and Tom leaned forward to watch. After a second, Robert pulled the stick out again.

"The tunnel's clear now," he said. "But we're letting in the cold air. I'd better put this in quickly, before they all freeze."

Rolling the bag neatly, he slid it into the tunnel. Then he reached for the stick and started to push. He had almost finished when Hope spoke from behind them, in her small, strange voice.

"Shhh," she said. And then again, "*Shhh*."

30

MR. ARMSTRONG WAS STANDING JUST BEHIND THEM, ON the other side of the ditch. He was looking at Hope.

"What have you done to her?" he said accusingly. "Why have you brought her here?"

"She's all right," Emma said. "We're looking after her. *We're* not going to shut her up in a hole."

Mr. Armstrong didn't bother to answer the taunt. "Get out of my way," he said. "I've come to take her home."

Hope was peering at his face in the half-light, watching every movement he made. Once or twice her mouth twisted soundlessly, copying one of his words. Tom saw her lips forming the shapes. *Here . . . get out . . . home . . .*

"I'm afraid you can't have her," Tom said. Very cool and polite. "We won't let her go back to that horrible place."

"I think there's been a misunderstanding," Mr. Armstrong said smoothly. "It was just a game. She likes to play hide-and-seek." He moved forward, to step across the ditch.

Emma stood up and blocked his way. "You don't expect us to believe that rubbish, do you? Go away, or we'll call the police."

Stupid, Tom thought. *Stupid, stupid*. It was a bad mistake to make him angry. What they had to do was keep him talking and spin things out as long as they could.

To give Lorn a chance to come out of the cavern.

Emma's dramatic gesture was completely pointless, anyway. Mr. Armstrong stepped straight over the ditch, pushing her away contemptuously. "Stop interfering," he said. "You don't know what you're talking about."

Emma staggered sideways, and Hope gave a funny little squeal. Then she thrust her fist into her open mouth so hard that Tom heard it thud against her teeth.

She's terrified of making a noise, he thought suddenly. *How did he teach her that? What did he do to keep her quiet under the floor?*

For the first time, he felt seriously frightened. All they knew about Mr. Armstrong was that he kept his daughter under the floor. And that his son was terrified of him. Now that they'd found Hope, he was in grave trouble. They had no idea how he might react to that or what he would do to get her back.

Tom wanted to lift her off the ground and run away, before any more horrible things could happen to her. But if he did that, they'd never get her back into the woods. They had to stay where they were, by the hedge bank. Waiting.

Why didn't Lorn come? Where was she?

Shuffling closer to Hope, Tom slid his arm around behind her, ready to hold on tight if there was any attempt to snatch her away. But Mr. Armstrong didn't lay a finger on her. Once he was over the ditch, he folded his arms and took a step back, staring down at them all. Hope looked away from him, gazing down at the nut she was holding.

"Stop that," Mr. Armstrong said. "Put that dirty thing down and come here."

Where is Lorn? Tom thought again. And then, worse, *Was it just a fantasy after all?*

Robert was still half turned toward the bank, trying to watch the cavern entrance without making it obvious. But Mr. Armstrong wasn't interested in him. All his attention was directed at Hope. She hadn't moved at all, except that her fingers had curled tightly around the nut, hiding it away.

"Come here," Mr. Armstrong said again. "Stand up and walk." This time there was an edge to his voice. A hint of something very cold and determined.

"I don't think she wants to," Tom said.

Mr. Armstrong didn't even glance at him. He was staring steadily at Hope, waiting for her to lift her head. Even from where he was sitting, Tom felt the brutal, unwavering force of that stare.

Hope felt it, too. After a second, she started trying to struggle out of the blankets. But she was very tired, and Robert had wrapped her up tightly, to keep her warm. The blankets tangled around her legs, and she put her head down and began to whine.

"Quiet," Mr. Armstrong said sharply. "Don't fuss."

Immediately, her hand came up and hit her face. Tom winced, but Mr. Armstrong hardly seemed to notice. He just went on waiting until Hope began to struggle again. Tom couldn't bear to watch. He reached over and loosened the blankets so that she could scramble out.

As she crawled free of them, Mr. Armstrong frowned and snapped at her again. "Stop that! Walk!"

Slowly and unsteadily, she hauled herself onto her feet. The ground was uneven and she wobbled slightly, spreading her arms for balance. She stood in a curious, unnatural way, with her knees turned outward so that all her weight was on the outside edges of her feet.

"Look at her," said Emma. "Poor little thing. She can hardly stand."

"She's lazy," Mr. Armstrong said coldly. "That's why I have to make her walk." He snapped his fingers and beckoned to Hope, and she took one shaky step forward.

Tom was shocked. Last time he'd seen her standing, they'd been desperate to get her away, with no time to notice what she looked like. Now he saw how she'd been affected by living under the floor. She was taller than he'd realized, but her body was pitifully slight and frail. Her head poked forward, and her spindly legs were awkward and ungainly. When she took her first step, she would have fallen if he hadn't jumped up and caught her.

As soon as he felt her weight against his hands, he knew he couldn't let Mr. Armstrong have her. Not even for a minute. Not even while they phoned the police. He could feel the narrow bones in her arms and the way her body trembled, and he knew she was afraid.

Lorn had to come. She *had* to. And he had to make sure that Hope was there to meet her.

He put his arms around her and swung her off the ground, holding her tightly. The dry clothes Emma had given her were wet now, too, and he could feel her shivering as she huddled against his chest. He looked at Mr. Armstrong over the top of her head.

"You're not having her," he said.

"Don't be ridiculous." Mr. Armstrong held out his hands. "She's my daughter. She belongs to me. Hand her over."

He said it like an adult giving orders to a stupid child. *Come on, now. That's enough of that. Stop playing games.* But behind that bullying, everyday impatience, Tom could hear something darker and more menacing. It took every scrap of determination he had to stay where he was, with Hope in his arms.

She was watching her father with a strange, detached expression, as though the argument had nothing to do with her. But both hands were jammed over her mouth, and she was trembling harder than before.

"Give me the blankets, Em," Tom said without looking around. "She needs wrapping up."

Emma scooped them up and draped them awkwardly around Hope's body, tucking them in where she could. Hope grabbed at the edges, and Tom saw her hunting for the plaited fringes and running her fingers up and down them, to feel the patterns she had made.

"Take your hands off her," Mr. Armstrong said. "She's mine."

Then, before Tom could answer, he lunged forward and grabbed at her body through the blankets. Tom was taken by surprise, but Hope reacted faster than he did. She flinched away from her father's hands, burying her face in Tom's chest.

Tom held on tightly, trying to pull her free. "Get off!" he said angrily.

For the first time, he raised his voice enough to carry beyond the woods. Immediately, on the other side of the hedge, Helga started to bark frantically. He could hear her tugging at her leash and rocking the bench on its concrete base.

Mr. Armstrong ignored that. He had a firm grip on Hope now. As he dug his fingers in and pulled, her mouth opened in what should have been a scream. But all that came out was a tiny, useless squeak.

"Leave her alone!" Emma shouted. "She doesn't want you!"

Tom peered through the leafless hedge, trying to spot someone who might come and help. But it was still too early. There was no one else in the park. Only Helga, barking and tugging at the bench. Tom knew he couldn't hold on to Hope much longer. Mr. Armstrong was dragging at her body with all his weight. If they both kept hold of her, she was going to get hurt.

Tom gave up on Lorn and shouted as loudly as he could. "Help! Is there anyone there? Come and help us!"

There was another burst of barking—and then a crash as the bench went over. Helga dragged her leash free and came straight for them, pushing her way through the hedge.

31

Lᴏʀɴ ʀᴀɴ ʙᴀᴄᴋ ᴅᴏᴡɴ ᴛʜᴇ ᴛᴜɴɴᴇʟs, ᴘᴀʏɪɴɢ ᴏᴜᴛ ᴛʜᴇ ʀᴏᴘᴇ as she went. When she reached the end of the first coil, she stopped for an instant to tie it to the beginning of the next one. Then she was away again, unwinding more rope.

All she wanted was to get back to Bando as fast as she could.

From the first bend in the tunnel, she could smell the earthsnakes and feel them twisting and squirming ahead of her. She had almost reached the place where they were when her ears caught a different sound. It was much fainter, and it came from behind her.

A quick scrabbling. Then silence. And then another scrabble.

She stopped dead, listening. There was another scrabble. Then a breath of air came drifting toward her, carrying the rank animal smell that pervaded all the tunnels. But this time it wasn't just a lingering scent, left behind on the surface of the earth. It was sharp and fresh and very strong. The smell of the creature itself.

The animal that had made the tunnels was coming up behind her, slowly but steadily. It didn't seem to have realized that she was there, but that could only be a matter of time. And there was nowhere to hide. Nothing to do but go forward—and try to reach Bando before it caught her.

She began to move again, not running now but creeping

softly and silently, terrified of making any noise in case the creature picked it up. For a moment she wondered whether to abandon the rope, but that seemed like giving up any chance of rescue. Without the rope, the others would never be able to follow her to the den. She went on uncoiling it, letting it fall quietly from her hand onto the soft earth floor.

There was another burst of scrabbling. This time it sounded closer, and the smell came at her in waves, making her want to retch. A panicky voice in her mind was screaming at her to run, run, RUN, not worrying where that would take her as long as it was away from the monster. But something deeper and more fearful kept her still and quiet.

No noise, said the voice in her head. *If you make noise, they'll come to get you. If you want to be safe, you have to go down. Go deeper. . . .*

She went around another bend and saw the patch of dim light where the earthsnakes were lying. They were still twined together, wriggling aimlessly on the floor of the tunnel. She couldn't believe that she had ever been afraid of them. It was easy to squeeze past, edging around their wet, looped bodies.

Once they were behind her, between her and the monster, she began to move more quickly, trusting that their movements would disguise any little noises she made. The monster was still a long way off, stopping and starting and stopping again. Still not concerned with anything she was doing.

Quietly . . . Go deeper. . . .

She went on uncoiling the rope and putting her feet down softly, step after step after step. And she was almost there, almost at the opening of the den where Bando was lying, when suddenly, without warning, the silence around her exploded.

There was a crash and a roar, and then the air was filled with deafening rumbles and thuds. The din came at her from all directions—from above, from ahead, and through the ground where she was standing. It shook her whole body, drowning out everything else for a moment.

Then it faded slightly—and she sensed the monster listening.

It was still now, and she heard it sniffing as it tested the air. It was what she did herself, and she could visualize exactly how it was moving, turning its head from side to side as it tried to find out what was going on.

It caught her scent.

For a telltale second, it froze, taking in the information. Registering a strange, unwelcome presence in its private territory. Then it sniffed again, not searching generally now but hunting for Lorn.

In the instant before it moved, she started to run.

She flung herself forward down the tunnel, with one hand against the wall to keep her on course. She could hear the monster charging after her, not scrabbling now, but racing down the tunnel at a speed that set the air swirling.

She had to reach Bando. She had to get to the den first.

There was nothing to lose by making a noise now. She shouted his name as loudly as she could.

"It's all right, Bando! I'm on my way! I'm nearly there!"

The sound told her exactly where she was, and another

ten steps took her to the opening of the den. She clutched at the wall to bring herself to a halt, and then dug both hands into it, scraping frantically until she found a strong loop of roots.

She slipped her last piece of rope through the loop, tying it on firmly. The end dangled over the black space below her. And she could hear the voice in her head, still saying the same things. *Go down, go deeper. You'll be safe if you go down. . . .*

But it wasn't true.

The voice that told her to go deeper didn't come from her own common sense. It was someone else's voice—a voice she was *remembering*. And it was wrong. There was no safety in going down. Once she was in the den, she would be trapped, with nothing to do except wait for the monster.

But she had to go down, all the same. Because Bando was down there, unconscious and maybe injured. She had to go down—even though she and Bando could only huddle together, waiting for the others to come. Hoping they'd arrive in time to help.

She had to be with him, to face whatever was going to happen.

Gripping the rope with both hands, she began to climb down, and the air grew colder as she went. When she landed, she found herself right beside Bando's body, and she reached out and touched his arm. It felt half frozen.

He stirred and mumbled something.

"It's all right," Lorn said soothingly. "I'm here now. And the others are on their way. It'll be all right."

She had no idea whether that was true or not. But she wasn't going to give up. Not yet. She sat down beside Bando and put a hand on his shoulder so that he would know where she was. Then she tilted her head back and listened as hard as she could.

32

HELGA FLEW INTO THE WOODS, FASTER THAN TOM HAD ever seen her run. One moment she was out on the grass, beyond the hedge. The next, she was flinging herself at Mr. Armstrong.

He lashed out sideways, trying to kick her away, but she dodged his foot and fastened her teeth in his trouser leg, tugging backward with all her strength. He shook her off once, but she came straight back, dancing around him and nipping at his ankle.

"Call it off," he snarled. "Get that dog away from me."

"Not unless you let go of Hope," Tom panted. "If you don't get your hands off her, I'll tell Helga to bite you."

He knew that Hope was frightened, because her eyes were screwed shut and her head was pushed hard against his chest, but he couldn't tell whether she was afraid of Helga or Mr. Armstrong. He tightened his aching arms around her body anyway, trying to calm down and breathe more slowly, to reassure her.

"It's all right," he muttered to the top of her head. "Hang on. We won't let you go."

Helga was still growling and snapping at Mr. Armstrong's legs, and he made another attempt to kick her. This time, he caught her in the ribs, and she went flying backward.

"You'll be sorry you did that," Robert said. He was on his

feet now, hovering protectively in front of the hedge bank. "I've never seen Helga quit."

As if she'd heard him, Helga came flying back and bit, hard, into the back of Mr. Armstrong's left calf. He yelped and stepped back, letting go of Hope at last.

"I'll get that dog destroyed!" he shouted.

"No, you won't," Tom said. "Because you dare not talk to the police." But he called Helga off. "Good, girl. That's enough. Sit."

Her ears went back, and she growled under her breath, but—after one reproachful glance—she sank back onto her haunches and sat there with her tongue hanging out, looking sideways at Mr. Armstrong.

He took a long breath and brushed the dust off his trousers. "Now, give me back my daughter," he said.

Tom had no intention of letting go of Hope, but he knew that he couldn't support her weight much longer. "Let's all sit down," he said. And he flopped onto the hedge bank, with Hope on his lap.

Mr. Armstrong looked down scornfully at him. "I have no intention of groveling," he said. His voice was still cold and even, but Tom could see sweat on his forehead. "And I won't have Hope sitting in the dirt either. She—"

Hope had her back to him now. She had opened her fist to look at the nut she was holding, and while he was still speaking, she lifted it toward her mouth.

"*I told you to throw that filthy thing away!*" Mr. Armstrong shouted.

He bent down and knocked her hand away from her face so that she dropped the nut onto the ground. With a small, desolate cry, she threw herself out of Tom's arms and onto the earth bank, pushing her fingers into the little pile of loose earth where the nut had fallen. The earth subsided, leaving a dip where there had been a little hummock.

And then it began to rise up again.

For a second, Tom thought his eyes had gone wrong. But when he blinked, the earth was still rising, coming back out of the ground like a little spring of water. As it formed itself back into the same little mound as before, he realized what it had to be.

So did Helga. She gave a loud, excited bark and threw herself forward onto the hummock.

"Leave it!" Tom said. "Leave it, Helga!"

But it was no use. Moles were the one thing she could never resist. She was already digging her way into the ground, throwing up a shower of loose earth behind her.

33

Lorn huddled beside Bando, listening to the world tearing itself to pieces. She could hear deep, thundering voices, like giants yelling at each other. And the unmistakable, terrifying sound of falling earth cascading down from the tunnel roof.

And, closer than that, she could hear the panting breath of the monster. It had almost reached the den now, and the temperature was starting to rise as its great warm body pushed down the tunnel toward them.

So many ways to die. So many ways of being eaten or suffocated or trampled to death. *I'll never understand now*, she thought. *There's no time left.* Memories were flooding into her head, but she would never make sense of them. She was going to die. Now. Deep under the ground.

But not without a fight.

It was a clear decision. Until then, she had been crouching passively, in the dark, next to Bando's unconscious body. Trying to shrink down into the soft litter of rotting leaves. But as the monster reached the entrance to the den, she struggled free of the leaves and shook Bando's shoulder, hard.

"Wake up!" she said loudly. "There's danger coming. It's time to fight."

He grunted and began to stir, but she didn't wait for him to come around. There was no time for that. Defiantly she scrambled to her feet, facing the opening above her head. She wasn't a warrior like Perdew or Ab. She had no kind of weapon except her bare hands. But she wasn't going to lie there meekly, waiting to be eaten. For as long as she could, she was going to fight.

She backed away until she felt solid ground behind her. Then she waited. There was still no light, but she could feel the baggy shape of the monster disturbing the air. She could hear the snuffling noise of its great, wet snout and the ugly scrabble of its nails. For a long second, she stood upright, trying to remember everything the hunters had ever said about how to find an animal's weakest point. She stood until the creature was there, above her, about to step down into the den. Until she could feel the heat of its foul breath on her face.

And then the roof fell in.

It came tumbling down around her, in a cloud of dust, tearing a ragged hole in the earth. There was a burst of light and a rush of freezing air, and Bando opened his eyes and screamed.

Above them was a monster a hundred times worse than the creature in the tunnel. And it was launching itself toward them with its huge yellow teeth bared to bite.

Tom grabbed at Helga's collar, pulling her away from the ground. But he wasn't quick enough to save the mole. Helga came up with it gripped between her teeth, shaking it ferociously from side to side.

"Poor little thing!" Emma said. "Put it down, Helga! Put it *down*—you'll frighten Hope."

But Hope wasn't looking at the mole. She was staring down intently at the ground, leaning forward to peer into the hole that Helga had made. And there was something in her face that made Emma bend toward her. That made Tom and Robert lean forward, too. They looked over Emma's shoulder, gazing into the earth.

Helga had dug down into the mole's sleeping chamber. The neat lining of grass and moss and leaves was covered with the earth she'd scattered as she burrowed through the roof. And there . . . on top of the earth . . . standing tiny and upright and impossible . . .

Tom knew who she was. He knew at once, even before Robert caught his breath. Because she *was* Hope. Even without the tangled braids and the pathetic, deformed limbs, she was the same person. The face that was turned up to look at them was the same as the face beside him, staring down.

They were vast and grotesque. Great giant figures, bending over the hole and crowding out the sky. Bando clutched at Lorn's hand, and for a second, she was like him, paralyzed with fear. Unable to think at all.

Then she caught a familiar scent.

Robert, she thought. *Oh, Robert, it's you—*

There was no change in what she saw above her, but something in her mind shifted, radically. All the faces hanging over her were still huge, but now one of them was *Robert's*. She'd thought she would never see him again, but he was there, looking down at her. Everything that Cam and Zak had said was true—but he was *there*.

She opened her mouth to call to him, but before she could

make a sound, one of the other faces moved, leaning closer. The movement stirred up the air, and the scent that came down to her this time was familiar, too.

But it wasn't a person. It was a place. . . .

Sitting on the earth, in the dark.
Down in the dark, to be safe. You have to stay down,
where no one will find you, where no one will see you.
You have to stay hidden.

But it's cold. . . .

The smell of that dark place was strong and unmistakable—but what was it doing out in the light, in the real world? How could it be there? *I don't understand,* she thought. *It doesn't make sense.*

And then her eyes slid away from Robert, following the scent. She saw the plaited hair hanging over her—and she *remembered*.

She remembered her fingers working in the dark, finding the beautiful patterns, one by one. Winding in every scrap of thread she could snatch, every possible strand of wool. She remembered the cold and the loneliness and the fear. And— as fierce and real as the icy air washing over her now—she remembered being on her own in the black room. For ever and ever.

That was her life. That was what she'd come from. And she knew she never wanted to go back there.

Every instinct told her to run away. It would be easy. All she had to do was grab Bando's hand and scramble up the fallen earth into the tunnel opening. The others were coming now—she could hear their voices somewhere in the distance—and she belonged in the cavern with them. In the place where she was *Lorn*. All she had to do was run and hide.

But . . .

The face that was hers and not hers was staring down at her. She could see the red marks on its cheeks where the hands had hit, punishing every sound. She could see its wary eyes and the skin of its scalp, pulled cruelly tight by the braids. And she remembered what it was to live that life. *If she only knew what I know*, she thought. *If she only understood. . . .*

It was impossible to run away. Impossible to hide that knowledge without sharing it. Slowly, standing on tiptoe, she reached up her hand.

Slowly, wonderingly, Hope stretched down into the earth, holding out one finger toward the tiny shape below.

Tom held his breath and bit his lip to stop himself from making any sound. *Let it work the right way*, he thought desperately. *Let Hope be free.*

He had forgotten about Mr. Armstrong. They'd all forgotten him. Nothing seemed real except the two hands moving to touch each other. The whole universe had shrunk to the tiny space between those outstretched fingers.

And then Mr. Armstrong grabbed.

He bent down and put his arms around Hope's body, gripping her hard through the blankets. Tom turned like lightning, furious with himself for being so careless. He seized Hope as well, not gently, but putting his whole weight into it. Desperate to keep her where she was, just for another second. Just long enough . . .

"Let go!" Mr. Armstrong spat. "She belongs to me!"

"You can't have her!" Tom said. "She's a *person*."

And then she was running away through their hands, like water through a funnel. Sliding and shrinking and disappearing, until they were left with nothing between them except a bundle of empty blankets and a few old clothes.

34

After what seemed a very long time, Mr. Armstrong began to feel the blankets, squeezing them stupidly and fumbling among the layers.

"Where is she?" he said.

"She's not here," said Emma, in a strange, uncertain voice. "You haven't got a daughter. Remember?"

Hope's empty clothes dropped out of the blankets and landed on the ground in a little heap. Tom looked down at them.

"There she is," he said. "Your nonexistent daughter." His voice was as shaky as Emma's. "Why don't you take *those* home and keep them under the floor?"

Mr. Armstrong picked the clothes up and shook them, looking bewildered. "Where has she gone? What have you done to her?"

"You were here," Robert said. "You saw the same as we did."

But Mr. Armstrong hadn't seen anything. They could tell that by the way he turned around, looking wildly into the woods. He didn't even glance at the ground in front of their feet or at the patch of raw earth where Helga had dug into the molehill. Instead, he stepped back over the ditch and began going back and forth through the trees, shouting Hope's name. They heard him calling for a long time, getting farther and farther away. Finally, there was the cough of an engine starting up in the parking lot, and the long gray car slid away, down the road.

When the sound had died away, Tom looked down at the hollow in the hedge bank. There was nothing there now. It was just a dip in the earth, lined with rotting leaves and moss.

All their attention had been focused on the empty blankets, on Mr. Armstrong's face, and his greedy, grabbing hands. While they were concentrating on those, Hope had slipped away from them. And the little figures at their feet had escaped back into the ground.

Helga came slinking back and put her nose into Tom's hand, and he patted her head absentmindedly.

"Did you see them go?" he said slowly. "Did you see *her*— after it happened?"

Emma shook her head. "I wasn't expecting anything like *that*."

"Nor was I," Robert said, still gazing down at the mole's empty den. "I thought I'd understand if I found Lorn. But it's worse. Why wasn't it the same for her as it was for me? What happened?"

"Do you think she's all right?" said Emma. "I mean—" Her words tailed away.

"How can we ever know?" Robert said bitterly. "If we'd been looking—if we'd *seen* her—we might have been able to tell. But it's too late now. We'll never know."

That's not right, Tom thought. Somehow, instinctively, he knew that Robert was wrong. But it took him a moment or two to figure out why he felt so sure.

When he did, he almost shouted for joy.

"We *do* know! Just think what happened. The minute she had a chance to get away, she took it. *Zap!* Hope wouldn't have done that. Not the way she was before. She'd still be there, sitting in the bottom of the hole."

"Yes." Emma nodded slowly, taking it in. "If she's escaped, then she's all right. And that means she's *Lorn.*" She looked up at Tom and a huge grin spread across her face. "We did it, didn't we? We saved her."

Robert nodded slowly. But he didn't smile. "We saved *Hope,*" he said. "But we haven't rescued *Lorn.* She's still down there in the cavern—and winter's almost here."

Emma patted his arm. "Don't worry, Rob. It'll be OK. We'll look after her."

Robert didn't reply. Tom looked at his stiff, miserable face for a moment. Then he knelt beside the hole, pushing Helga away when she tried to join him. "Here's one thing we can do right now," he said.

He started to scoop the earth back into the hole, blocking off the end of the tunnel. After a few seconds, Robert knelt next to him and began to help, patting the loose earth flat as it was shoveled in.

Tom waited until they'd almost finished. Then he leaned sideways and muttered, very softly, "We had to do it, Robbo. You know that as well as I do."

Robert picked up a handful of dead leaves and scattered them over the patch of earth he'd just flattened. "I suppose so," he said under his breath. "But why does it have to be so *hard*?" His mouth twisted and he turned away, hiding his face from Tom.

For once in his life, Tom didn't try to give an answer. He

just waited. It took a while, but at last Robert looked back at him.

"Well, there's one good thing, anyway," he said lightly.

Tom raised his eyebrows. "What's that?"

"You believe me now. I finally got you to change your mind about something. That has to be a first."

Tom made a face at him. "Don't count on doing it again." Then he grinned and raised his voice, making sure Emma could hear. "Anyway, there's a much better first coming up soon."

"Oh yes?" Emma had stepped across the ditch, away from them. But she took the bait—just as Tom had meant her to. "What's that, then?"

Tom looked up at her, innocently. "Well, we'll have to go home and change now, won't we? We're all pretty muddy. And that means—" His grin widened. "You're going to be *late for school*, Emma Doherty!"

For an instant he thought she was going to shout at him. Then she glanced down at her watch and grinned back. "You want to bet?"

Before either of the others could reply, she had jumped across the ditch and started to run. She was out of the woods and on the grass before they caught up with her.

"Once upon a time," Zak said, "there was a man whose baby daughter died."

No, Lorn thought. *No, I don't want to hear this.*

The words connected with the angry, ugly memories that filled her mind. They were all sliding together now, making a dark pattern, full of pain and grief. She still didn't understand everything, but she remembered now. She *knew*. And it was almost too much to bear.

How could Zak be asking her to cope with more?

She wanted to crawl away and curl up in a shadowy corner. But that would be going backward. Retreating into another dark corner, on her own. She was *Lorn*, and her place was in the circle. So she sat still, like the others, listening.

Zak's face was tired and lined in the firelight. "The man couldn't stop his daughter from dying," he said. His hands moved over the drum on his lap, not making any sound. "The doctors and nurses and social workers and experts came and took her away from his house. She was his, but they shut her away inside a hospital and stuck her full of needles and tubes and medicines. And when she died, they said to the man, *It's your fault*."

On the other side of the circle, Bando suddenly lifted his head. He was lying on the stretcher they had used to bring him back along the tunnels—a length of thick white cloth wound tightly around two heavy wooden posts. No one knew what it was, but it had appeared in the cavern like magic, just when they needed it to carry him back along the tunnels.

He still looked pale and dazed, but that didn't stop him from interrupting the story. "It's not fair!" he said indignantly. "They were the ones who took her away. How could it be the man's fault if she died?"

The left side of Zak's mouth curled up into a half smile. "That's just what the man said. *It's not my fault*. He blamed the doctors for not saving his daughter's life. He blamed the nurses and the social workers and the experts. *She belonged to me, and they took her away and killed her.*"

He stroked the drum skin, and it murmured softly under his fingers. They all waited for him to go on, but he didn't speak. After a moment, Perdew prompted him impatiently.

"What happened next?"

Zak stroked the drum skin again. "For a long, long time nothing happened at all. Only the voice in his head, shutting out everything else. *It wasn't my fault. . . . It wasn't my fault. . . .* For years and years and years. And then—"

"And then?" Annet said, leaning forward eagerly.

Zak's fingers began to beat out a slow, insistent rhythm. "And then," he said, "the man had another daughter. . . ."

Lorn wanted to block her ears. She wanted to shut out his voice. But she knew she had to hear the story. She put her hands in her lap, knotting her fingers together to keep them there while she listened.

Because she could hear it now. She was ready to understand.

35

Tom almost made it to school in time. As the last bend came into view, he saw Robert and Emma ahead of him, running flat out. Robert glanced back over his shoulder, and when he saw Tom, he stopped to wait for him. Emma went on, flying around the corner at top speed.

So she wasn't going to be late after all. Well, if she could do it—so could he. Tom broke into a run, determined to beat the bell.

"Come on!" he said as he passed Robert. "Let's catch her!"

In two strides Robert was beside him. The two of them raced around the corner together—

—and bumped into a man coming the other way.

Tom cannoned straight into him, knocking himself off balance. He staggered sideways, and if he hadn't caught hold of Robert's arm, he would have fallen into the gutter.

"Sorry," Tom said, looking up apologetically.

In the same moment, Robert caught his breath. "You?" he said. "Aren't you the one—?" And then he broke off, without finishing.

The man didn't speak at all. He just stood still, looking straight back at Tom. And his eyes were as clear as water, as blue as a cloudless sky.

I've seen you before, said a voice inside Tom's head. But he couldn't think when or where. All he could do was stare at his own reflection in the center of those blue eyes while the man looked gravely back at him.

He didn't know how long he went on staring. It could have been for a split second or for an hour. While it lasted, there was nothing except the bright, dazzling blue.

And then, suddenly, it was over. The man stepped past them and disappeared around the corner, and they heard the school bell begin to ring.